DANCING WITH EVIL

Sheryll O'Brien

This is a work of fiction. All characters in this book are the product of an overactive imagination. Any businesses, organizations, places, events, and incidents are used fictionally. Any resemblance to a real person, living or dead, is a tremendous coincidence.

ISBN: 978-1-939351-54-8

WOODWIND PRESS

Printed in United States of America

For a complete list of Sheryll O'Brien books

Please visit her website:

www.pullingthreadsnovella.com

DANCING WITH EVIL

Sheryll O'Brien

~~ 1 ~~

Open your eyes.
Open your eyes.
Open your eyes.
Dozens of times, those words flitted through her brain, and dozens of times, she found it impossible to obey.
Open your eyes.
Open your eyes.
Open your eyes.
When her eyes finally popped open, bright light streaming through her bedroom window assaulted them shut. Instantly blinded by searing flashes of light and oddly shaped swirls and twirls, she eagerly sought shelter behind heavy, swollen lids. All too soon, her psychedelic light show lost both its edge and its allure, prompting her to seek daylight, once again. Ever so cautiously, she eased her battle-weary eyes open and peeked out into the world through a mass of fluttering lashes.

Much like a wounded animal, she lay there for a minute or two, maybe an hour or two, taking in her surroundings. All the while, she struggled to lift her head from her pillow. Unable to manage the weight of her own head, she moved on to her limbs. First, she tried to move her arms and hands. Then she worked on her legs and feet. Finding they too felt as though they had been weighted down, she rested a minute before trying once again. When once again came and went, it came and went with only a flicker of movement in her belligerent lot of her extremities.

Failing to rouse her semi-paralytic frame, she proceeded to a new set of failures. Those surrounding her inability to keep pesky little thoughts from swarming through her mind. Swarming as though they had been carried on the wings of a thousand angry bees. Swarming bees, stinging bees, asking bees.

What time is it?

What time is it?

Rolling her head, she found the bedroom clock with her eyes, fought hard against an internal fog to focus on the bright red numbers.

One-twenty.

You have to get up! You told Page and Preston that you would pick them up from school today. Get up! Get up!

Willing her body to obey her command brought her nothing but defeat. Demanding it obey, quickly turned that defeat into a state of utter despair. With tears streaming down her face, she tried once more to move. And once more, she failed.

Locking on to her only link to the outside world, she watched as the bright red numbers on her digital clock flipped past. Able to do little more than register the minutes as they slipped quietly away, she held the numbers in her foggy gaze, blinking only when one number faded to the next.

One-twenty-three.

Blink.

One-twenty-four.

Blink.

One-twenty-five.

Blink.

Desperation mounting, she tried once more to move. This time she managed to pull herself to the edge of the bed. Managed to run a litany of instructions through her feeble brain as well.

Call the school. Tell them to have Page and Preston wait. Tell them not to take the bus. Tell them mommy will be there, just like she promised.

Collapsing back onto the bed, she tried reaching for the telephone. Spasm-like contractions running along her rubbery arms caused her to lose control of her hand. With her efforts to reach the phone, she knocked her favorite picture of Page and Preston off the nightstand and onto the floor.

With one arm wrapped tightly around a bedpost, she directed her dangling limb toward the picture frame. The spinning whirling picture frame that laid just beyond her reach. Anchoring herself against a sturdy mahogany bedpost, she tried to stem the violent throbbing in her head and calm the whirling dervish that had taken up residence in her stomach. Exhausted from her efforts, she collapsed flat onto the mattress and sacrificed herself to the swarm of bees that were hell-bent on delivering another message.

Something is wrong! Help! Get help!

Reaching for the phone, she struggled to pull the receiver to her. A sudden jerk of her arm caused the receiver to bang heavily against her forehead. Before she could even register the painful thump that echoed through her cavernous skull, the bees came back. Swarming, stinging, asking.

What's wrong?

What's wrong?

Focusing on the phone, she pushed the talk button, then the tiny numbers before collapsing once again.

~~ 2 ~~

Racing down the crowded Hall toward his sister, Preston purposefully bumped against her as she pulled on her raincoat.

"Cut it out, Pres!"

"Come on, Page. Hurry! I want to get a good seat on the bus."

"We're not taking the bus. Mom's coming to pick us up today. Re-mem-ber?"

"If Mom's not waiting for us outside, we're supposed to take the bus. Re-mem-ber?"

"Mom will be waiting."

"Maybe. Maybe not."

"She promised me. She'll be here. You'll see." Too eager for words, Preston pulled Page along the crowded school corridor. Banging and bumping her way behind her bossy older brother, Page shouted her apologies to those she battered and bruised along the way.

Abandoning his sister at the main door, Preston made a mad dash toward the bus, shouting over his shoulder for his sister to follow him.

"Page, come on. Mom's not here!"

Standing her ground, Page scanned the bustling horseshoe driveway for her mother's van. Hoping against hope that her mother would arrive before she had to step foot on the bright yellow bus, Page dug her tiny heels into the top step. Refusing to budge until the very last moment, Page turned a watchful eye toward the protective green and white striped awning that shielded her from tiny remnants of that morning's storm, and from an unseasonably raw blast of post-winter wind. Distracted by the noisy flicker-flicker-flap of the awning's ruffled edge, Page rewarded herself with a momentary reprieve from the despair that the impending bus trip caused her. Tuning out the world, Page silently recited that day's hopeful little mantra.

She said she would come today. She'll come.

I know she'll come. She said she would come today. She will come.

But when the first of the buses inched their way from the schoolyard, Page accepted her fate. Accepted that she was going to have to take the bus home, and as her grandmother had always said, there were no ifs, ands, or buts about it. Disappointed by her mother's unfilled promise, Page slowly made her way toward the bus, climbed its mud-soaked stairs, and plopped into a seat halfway back. Looking past her fellow commuters, Page searched for Preston, relaxed a bit when she found him in his usual spot, way in the back with all the big kids.

At least I'm on the right bus this time.

Pushing in along her seat, Page pressed her sad little face against the rain dotted window and search for her mother once more. Finding her mother nowhere in sight, Page felt the familiar ping of disappointment as it struck a hollow chord in her heart. She heard the painfully familiar chant she had recited countless times before begin anew.

Come on Mom. Please!
Please don't make me take the bus, please!
I hate the bus, Mom. Please!

When the doors of the bus whooshed closed and the bright yellow tin-can jerked forward, reality hit sweet little Page. Her mother **wasn't** coming to pick her up that day. Her mother **wasn't** going to keep her promise. Closing her eyes to the world, Page welcomed the silent tears that slid down her cheeks. When the last tear dropped from her sad little face, Page recited the final stanza of her woeful chant.

But you promised, Mom.
You promised.
And you broke your promise, Mom.
Again!

~~ 3 ~~

Page hated the bus. Hated everything about it. The starting, the stopping, the smell, the noise.

Preston on the other hand, loved the bus and Page knew why. Turning in her seat, Page watched as Preston horsed around with a group of kids. It didn't matter that the kids were bigger, or older, or more smart mouth than Preston. No, all that mattered was that Preston fit in with the group on the bus ... or the group at the ball field ... or any other group he found himself a part of. Even though Page had never been part of a group, she knew what being part of a group meant. It meant that you were accepted. It meant that you mattered. Most of all, it meant that you would have someone to horse around with on the way home from school. Just like Preston.

Staring at the far end of the bus, Page admitted for the first time ever, that she wanted someone to horse around with. But when she looked to her left, all she found was an empty seat. While sitting all alone made her sad, the memory of Preston's hurtful words that morning made her even sadder.

"You only hate taking the bus, Page, because you always sit alone. And you only sit alone, because you don't have any friends."

Desperate for someone to sit with, Page scanned the bus for someone ... **anyone** ... who might be sitting without a seat partner. Finding the only empty seat on the bus was next to her, Page gave up her search and pulled her heavy backpack from the floor. Placing it onto the seat next to her, Page watched in horror, as the muddy backpack left giant mud trails along the empty seat.

Great! Now nobody will sit next to me. Ever!

Wiping the seat with her jacket sleeve only made things worse, so Page stopped her cleaning and pulled open her backpack. She dug deep inside and retrieved her reading book and glasses. Before delving into chapter 4 of *Dear God, it's me Margaret,* Page checked Preston one more time. Catching Preston's less than friendly wave in a jumble of flailing arms and legs, Page quickly answered his greeting with a timid wave of her own before opening her book.

As Page was nearing the end of chapter 6, the bus was nearing the end of its trip. If there was any part of the bus trip that Page enjoyed, she decided this might be it. Most of the kids had already been dropped off at their stops, so the bus was left practically empty. Empty and quiet. Quiet enough so that Page only had to read each page of her book once to understand it. Empty enough so that she wasn't the only kid who sat alone in the bright yellow tin can. With her nose pressed tightly into her book, Page pretended to read on. Instead, she thought about her mother.

Five more stops then I'll be home. I can't wait to see you, Mom. Mom, why didn't you come pick us up today? Or yesterday? Or last week? You used to pick us up. It used to be different. You used to be different.

The sudden stop of the school bus startled Page from her thoughts.

The shouting that echoed through the bright yellow tin can scared her.

Looking toward the front of the bus, Page soon learned what all the shouting was about. The bus had stopped practically on top of a truck, and the bus driver seemed mad. Really mad. With her window open, the bus driver yelled at the driver of the truck.

"Move! Move that thing! I've got kids on this bus! Get back in your truck and move it!"

Page had heard the driver yell before, but never at someone outside the bus, and never in such a stern way. Usually, the driver's harshest words were directed at Preston and his friends, and truth be told, her words really weren't so mean. Certainly not as mean sounding as the ones currently spilling forth.

"What's wrong with you man? Move that damn rig. I've got kids in here!"

Before the bus driver stopped her yelling, A chorus of yells erupted from behind Page. The tone of the voices, and the laughter echoed loud and clear, Page wondered what all the commotion was about. Twisting in her seat, Page found Preston and two other boys standing at the back door waving at something. Raising herself up, Page strained over the tall bus seats to see what the excitement was about.

"Big deal," she whispered as she caught sight of a truck stopped tight against the back of the bus. "Another stuck truck. What's the big deal?"

Being wedged between two trucks seemed less than thrilling to Page, but the commotion that Preston and his friends were causing was thrilling. Caught in the merriment of the final few kids on the bus, and almost feeling as though she were part of it, Page watched as Preston and his friends motioned for the truck driver to honk his horn. When the driver complied with a friendly honk ... honk, Page dropped back into her seat and laughed. Continued laughing until she heard another round of Screams followed by a series of less than friendly honk ... honk ... honks!

Turning toward the back of the bus again, Page found that Preston and his friends had moved away from their usual spot. Pushed deep into seats of their own, the boys banged fiercely against closed bus windows and waved their arms frantically, as blood-curdling screams echoed throughout the bright yellow tin can.

Spinning nearly out of her seat, Page looked out her window at the oncoming headlight of a train as it barreled toward the school bus she wasn't supposed to be on that day. The school bus that sat stranded between two trucks on a set of railroad tracks. The school bus she hated.

Panic racing through her, Page turned toward Preston one last time. With only seconds to spare, she managed a pitiful little scream for the two people who mattered most to her in the whole wide world.

"Preston! Mommy!"

Making it to his sister's seat just before the train did, Preston pulled Page close so she wouldn't die all alone on the half empty school bus seat.

~~ 4 ~~

Reverend Dawson slowly made his way around ebony draped mourners toward tiny twin caskets beautifully flanked by spring's sweet floral treasures. Struggling with the weight of the grieving, the reverend mumbled through a graveside prayer that included a few too many references to God, and his merciful plan, for her liking. Seeking refuge in the hollow abyss that was once her mind, she managed to zone out until the reverend scattered a handful of dirt across the sinfully small shiny white boxes and uttered a final "ashes to ashes and dust to dust". Finding there was no shelter from the horrific reality of those words, she leaned against the dark clad man supporting her.

Aroused by a gentle nudge on her elbow she willed her zombie-like body toward her children's caskets. With trembling fingers, she reached out and placed a single yellow rose bound with plumes of baby's breath at the spot where she imagined her children's hearts would be. Then as any mother would, she left a tender goodbye kiss for each of her sweet babies. Marking for all eternity the head of each casket with a soft, pale pink lipstick kiss, she lingered a moment as precious memories flooded her. Memories of lipstick kisses she had left on notes she often tucked inside her children's lunch boxes or under their pillows at night. Memories of lipstick kisses she would find smeared across her Mother's Day cards.

Running her hands along the cool silky coffins, she bent low and whispered her children's good night prayer one final time, "God bless you, I love you, good night, Page. God bless you, I love you, good night, Preston.

Unable to stop the world ... her world ... from spinning out of control, she took hold of the sturdy hand offered her, then took her first step away from the eternal resting place of her reasons for living.

As though devoured by the massive funeral limousine, she pressed herself into the deep rich leather seat, and pulled her grief tight around her. Staring blankly at the well-meaning 'talking heads' across from her she forced herself to listen to their plans.

"Denny will go home to rest. Denny doesn't need to worry about a thing. If Denny feels she's up to company we will let Reverend Dawson know."

By the time the car inched its way out of the cemetery, her feeble mind could barely register the Denny ... Denny ... Denny part of each sentence. Unable, or unwilling to respond to the outside world, Denny remained silent. Inside, however, a blood curdling scream resonated through her body, her mind, her soul.

I want my children! Please God, I need my children!

Resting her head against the cool dark window, she closed her eyes and begged her grief to wash over her. Unfortunately, her anguished tears did nothing to cleanse her of her pain, or of her guilt.

When a bright morning sun kissed her awake the next day, she felt his presence. When darkness crept into the corners of her room that night, she felt his presence. It was the same thing for days on end.

Bright Morning Sun.

Evening Darkness.

His presence in between.

Bright Morning Sun.

Evening Darkness.

His Tender Touch. His words of love.

Then one day only bright morning sun and evening darkness was there. He had gone away. She still heard him. Heard his tender words of encouragement, tender words of love.

"Hi honey, it's me. I'm sorry I had to leave. Honey, I hope you're okay. If you're okay, could you pick up the phone? Please. Maybe you're sleeping. Okay, I'm at work if you need me. Just call if you need me. Okay? Just call. I love you. Bye."

After the 5th telephone message, after the 5th I love you, Denny pulled the phone's plug from the wall and retreated into her own little world. Her quiet, peaceful little world of memories.

~~ 5 ~~

Silently, he crawled into bed each night, and silently, she welcomed him. She needed him, she wanted him, but she had hurt him. So, this night she waited patiently for his breathing to take on a sleeping rhythm, and when it did, she left their bed.

Having been cooped up in her bedroom for days on end, she chose this night to venture out into the hall. Alone with her thoughts, she turned toward her children's rooms, stopping cold when a razor-sharp blade of grief stabbed at her heart. Desperate to be near her children, she placed one rubbery leg in front of the other and moved silently down the hall. A hall she had traveled hundreds of times before. A hall that suddenly seemed impossible to travel. Dropping to her knees she let out a wretched moan before screaming out for her children.

"Page! Pres!"

Swept from the floor, she collapsed into the powerful arms that held her close. Burying her face against her husband's neck, she let a river of tears wash over them.

"Cliff ... the kids."

"I'm here, Denny. Shhh. It's alright. Everything will be alright. Shhh."

Sobbing and gasping for air, she repeated her children's names over and over and over.

"Page. Pres. Page. Pres. Ohhhh ... Page ... Pres ..."

Clinging to one another for the first time since their children's deaths, Cliff and Denny Jameson shared their profound grief. Shared the horror of a parent's worst nightmare. There on the warmly carpeted hallway floor, they nestled in each other's arms and grieved together.

Denny spent the rest of that night wrapped in the protective embrace of her husband. Unable to sleep, and desperate to escape her feelings of despair, she turned her attention to the bright red numbers on her digital clock. Mindlessly, she watched as minutes slowly surrendered to that vastness known as wasted time.

Wasted time. I wasted time. With Page. With Pres. I'm wasting it now with Cliff.

Backing herself tight against her husband, Denny waited for the slightest stir, the slightest connection between them. Receiving none, she settled once again into the dark around her. When the morning's bright sun announced a new day, Cliff greeted it well rested. Denny on the other hand, just rolled over and withdrew from her world.

Cliff Jamison left his wife that morning where he found her the day before, where he was sure he would find her again that evening.

Open your eyes.
Open your eyes.
Someone's here. Open your eyes!
Voices coming from off in the distance pulled Denny from her peaceful slumber. Focusing on the voices, she soon realized where they were coming from, realized whose they were.

Cliff and Susan.
Desperate for some human interaction, Denny dragged herself from the bed. Stumbling a bit on wobbly legs, she righted herself against the bedpost, before moving out into the hallway. Denny made her way to the staircase then using the wall for support, she slid her back downward, until she lowered herself onto the top stair. Pulling her trembling knees to her chest, then she wrapped her arms tightly around them and listened.

"Cliff honey, you've got to do something to help Denny."

"I don't know what to do, Mom."

"Get her to a doctor. Maybe get a prescription or something."

"Drugs? You think she needs drugs?"

"Medicine, Cliff. Honestly all you police officers think about are drugs. Medicine and drugs are two different things you know."

"Really? Well, I've seen plenty of people hooked on *medicine* and I've seen plenty of people hooked on *drugs.* From where I stand, they look the same."

"Denny is not going to get hooked on anything Cliff. We will make sure of that. "

Weary from the human interaction going on below her, Denny pulled herself to her feet. She turned and headed toward her children's bedrooms. Stopping at Page's room first, Denny ran her fingertips over the delicately scripted lettering on the door.

*Page Susan Jameso*n

Page had been so filled with joy when she first laid eyes on her new door. She had been so pleased with her room, her space, her place away from her taunting, teasing older brother. The door with the pastel floral stencil soon became a symbol of what Page wanted from the world, of what she offered to it. When she wanted her solitude, her fantasies, her dreams, she closed the world out from her haven. When she wanted relief from her solitude, her aloneness, she opened it wide offering herself to the world and all its possibilities.

Denny turned the antique glass door knob and gently pushed Page's door open. Recoiling from the soft filtered light that greeted her Denny gulped hard at the bitter bile that rose from the bowels of hell.

Page's night light. It's on. Why is it on? Maybe, oh God please, maybe this was a dream a horrible, horrible dream.

Turning pleading eyes toward the whimsical night light, Denny woefully abandoned the maybes as she desperately stole whatever comfort she could from the fairy that stood guard over Page's things.

She's waiting for you Page. See, Esmeralda is waiting for you to come home. Please come home Page, please!

After several minutes of gut-wrenching pain had passed, then she moved further into Page's room. Closing the door behind her, she breathed in deeply. Pulling the sweet, tender scent of her daughter into her shattered heart, Denny softly whispered a plaintive plea that cut through the stillness.

"Page. My sweet, sweet Page. Please come home. Mommy needs you. Tell God that Mommy needs you. Please baby, come home."

Enormous, salty tears cut through her, confirming in the most painful way that this was not a dream. Blinded by angry, stinging tears, and wounded to her core, Denny forced herself to stay near Page's things ... near Page. The pain, finally too much to bear, sent Denny into a heap on her daughter's pink and white striped comforter. Pulling her baby girls teddy bear, Mrs. Beasley from beneath her, Denny hugged it tight as the most painful of all realities hit her. Page's teddy bear wasn't nestled close to her daughter. Page was all alone in the cold dark ground.

"Mrs. Beasley. Oh Mrs. Beasley, you should be with Page. I should have told Cliff to put you with Page. You should be with her. Forever. She needs you."

Cliff and Susan escorted a completely destroyed Denny from Page's room. After tucking her safely in bed, they kept the silent vigil by her side.

When bright morning sun whispered promises of a new day, Cliff announced that he had come to a decision.

"I'll call the doctor, Mom. Maybe he can come by. Maybe he can help her."

"And what about you Cliff, who's going to help you?"

"Don't worry about me, Mom. When Denny's taken care of, I'll be all right."

~~ 6 ~~

Dr. Valez spent more than an hour with Denny. Poking, prodding, asking questions, offering words of condolence and reassurance. Denny barely noticed. The most she could do was stare blankly past the worrisome eyes that searched her body for signs of life. Susan, on the other hand, noticed his compassion and his skill.

"It's so kind of you to come, and to spend so much time with Denny."

"Mrs. Jameson, your daughter-in-law is in rough shape."

Susan nodded. "Grief is a powerful enemy."

"As is depression. I'm afraid that's what we're looking at here."

Pulling a prescription pad from his medical bag, Dr. Valez scribbled something illegible across the top slip and handed it to Mrs. Jameson.

"First, I'd like the patient to get some rest. Just because she's been in bed for over a week doesn't mean she's been sleeping. I've prescribed a mild sedative. It should help. "

Moving toward the door, Dr. Valez continued, "I'll stop by next week and check on her. Probably prescribe an antidepressant, and maybe refer her to a grief counselor. Until then, push fluids all day. Talk to her. Even if she doesn't respond, it's important to keep her connected. "

Cliff found a sleeping Denny in Preston's room that night. After he led her back to bed, he gave her a white oval shaped pill and a glass of water.

"The doctor says it will help you sleep."

Denny took the pill and laid back against her pillow. In the dark, quiet room, she waited and waited and waited. Sleep, however, didn't rescue her. No matter how she pleaded, it hid just beyond the edges of her mind. It eluded her, played with her, tormented her. Even so, the pill Cliff had given her helped her relax and it mercifully stemmed the throbbing in her head.

When Susan checked in on Denny the next morning, she found her fully awake.

"How did you sleep last night? Any better? "

Moving around Denny's room, Susan checked for the slightest response. As usual, she received nothing but a blank stare from her daughter-in-law.

"Did you take your pill this morning?"

Again, Denny gave nothing.

"You'll probably nod off soon. I know, why don't I just sit here for a while and do a little knitting, maybe we can watch Regis and Kelly together. Would that be all right?"

To that suggestion, Denny nodded. At least Susan thought she nodded.

Bright Morning Sun.
Evening Darkness.
Bright Morning Sun.
Evening Darkness.

In between, there were countless white oval shaped pills, and very little else.

Denny was seated in a rocking chair when Dr. Valez arrived a week later.

"Well, you certainly look better. "

Silently, Denny tolerated the doctor's exam. When he finished, Susan helped Denny back to bed, as they listened to the doctor's opinion.

"She's still pretty weak. Has she been taking her pills? Getting rest? "

Susan nodded.

"Good. Let's continue the sedative for another couple of days, then begin the anti-depressant. It may take a few days for her body to adjust so watch her for any signs of mania or deeper depression."

That evening, the white oval shaped pills she had been taking were replaced with shiny purple pills.

"These should help you feel better," Cliff and Susan said as they popped a pill into her mouth.

Denny's thoughts were like screams in her mind. Don't you get it. I don't want to feel better. I don't want to feel anything!

And for countless days, she didn't.

For countless days, Denny slept. Power slept.

Soon, sleep became Denny's friend. Her solace. Her lover. It welcomed her with open arms, then wrapped its loving embrace around her. It forbade her to move, to think, to feel. Occasionally, sounds from the outside world broke through her peaceful slumber. Occasionally, she focused on the sounds ... Raindrops pitter-pattering ... Birds chirping ... Dogs barking ... Voices interrupting.

"Cliff, the doctor said it might take a few days for Denny to adjust to the anti-depressant, but this just seems wrong."

"What do you mean?"

"Look at her. All she does is sleep."

"She must need it."

"Do you think we should call the doctor?"

"If she doesn't snap to in a few more days, we can call. Okay?"

Nodding, Susan tentatively broached another subject. "You know, Cliff, Denny wasn't herself even before the accident."

"Mom please, not now."

"If not now Cliff, when?"

His back ramrod straight, Cliff stormed to the bedroom window.

Desperate to reach her son, Susan tried once more. "Maybe whatever was wrong with Denny before, is adding to her grief. Maybe she needs more than pills."

"Like what, mom? "

"Maybe therapy would help. "

"Therapy?"

As was expected, Cliff scoffed at the word, at the very notion of therapy. Susan knew going in, that therapy would be a tough sell. After all, she had seen enough Oprah episodes to know that men generally hated the idea of therapy. And tough men, like cops, firefighters, soldiers, well they didn't bother hating the idea because they wouldn't even entertain the idea in the first place.

Completely convinced that therapy was what Denny needed, Susan pushed the issue. "Cliff, Denny needs to talk to someone."

Pointing to his wife, Cliff argued, "Have you seen Denny lately, Mom? She's not talking. Not to me. Not to you. Not to anyone."

"Maybe a professional could get through to her."

"The medication will get through to her. We will get through to her. Case closed!"

With that, Cliff stormed from the bedroom, leaving his mother as eerily silent as his near lifeless wife.

~~ 7 ~~

Susan was immediately put through to Dr. Valez.

"Mrs. Jameson what can I do for you? "

"For Denny actually, Dr. Valez I was wondering if you could recommend a counselor."

"A grief counselor?"

Thinking back to Denny's irregular behavior before the accident, and then to the lifeless form wasting away in a bed of grief, Susan stated her real needs. "A counselor who knows about grief, certainly, but someone who can help Denny put her life back together. Whatever that may entail."

"You mean a therapist. Yes, of course. Working through her grief is only the beginning for Denny, isn't it? "

"Yes, I'm afraid so."

Folding the piece of paper she had written the therapist's name and number on, Susan paced the spotless kitchen. As she paced, she debated.

Maybe I shouldn't call. Cliff doesn't want me to but, Denny needs help. This isn't about Cliff, it's *about Denny. Still, she is Cliff's wife, and **he** should decide what's best for her. And **I** should support his decisions. Especially after everything that's happened.*

When Susan checked on Denny that afternoon, she knew that she had to get Denny help. She knew that she would get Denny help; no matter what Cliff thought, or said. By mid-afternoon, Susan had worked up the courage to place the call. Unfortunately, her efforts were only marginally rewarded by an answering machine message.

"You've reached the office of Beth Malone. Unfortunately, I am unable to take your call. Please leave your name, number, and reason for calling, at the tone. If this is an emergency, please go to the nearest emergency room, otherwise I'll return your call within 24 hours."

Not wanting Beth Malone to call her at Cliff's, Susan left her name and her home phone number. Finished her call by asking that Dr. Malone call her at home that evening.

As Susan willed herself to sleep later that night, her brief conversation with Beth Malone played over and over in her weary mind.

"Mrs. Jameson, I spoke with Dr. Valez earlier, and he explained the situation with your daughter-in-law. How tragic. You have my deepest sympathies."

"Thank you. "

"The doctor said you would likely be interested in arranging home visits."

"Yes, please."

"Thursdays from 10:00 to 11:00 would work well for me. Is that convenient for you?"

"Yes, Thursdays would work fine."

"Good. Why don't we get the business requirements out of the way now. Do you have a few minutes?"

"Yes, now would be fine. "

"Good. Mrs. Jameson, what is your daughter-in-law's name?"

"Denny Jameson."

"And her husband's name?"

"Why do you ask? You don't need him to be a part of this do you?"

"Well, at some point probably."

"Oh, I see."

"Is that going to be a problem, Mrs. Jameson?"

"Cliff, Denny's husband, he doesn't think Denny needs therapy. Actually, he thinks therapy is a bunch of hogwash."

As though she hadn't heard the insult, Dr. Malone moved on. "How will you explain my visits then?"

"Cliff isn't around during the day. So, there is really no need to tell him that you're seeing Denny. If there's any progress to report, then I will tell Cliff about your visits. He could hardly say anything negative about therapy, if Denny's better. If there's no improvement with Denny, then Cliff doesn't need to know we even tried therapy."

"Mrs. Jameson, I'm sure you want to help your daughter-in-law but do you think this is the best way of going about it?"

Choking back tears, Susan whispered, "Unfortunately, I'm afraid it's the only way. "

That Thursday morning, Susan woke a bundle of nerves. She was concerned about the therapist getting in and out of the house without Cliff knowing. She worried during her drive to Cliff's house, and was still worried to the point of distraction while she took care of Denny's morning needs. Because of her distraction, while carrying a barely touched breakfast tray from Denny's room, she bumped full force into Cliff in the upstairs hallway.

"Hey Mom, where's the fire?"

"What? Oh, I'm sorry. Did I get anything on you?"

"No, no I'm fine. That's more than I can say for you?"

"What? "

"Are you all right? You look a little flustered. "

"Me? Flustered? Really?"

"Really."

"I must be a little distracted, that's all."

"About?"

"Denny, of course."

Scanning Denny's breakfast tray, Cliff asked, "How'd she do?"

"She just picked."

"So I see."

"Cliff, aren't you going to be late for work?"

Checking his watch, Cliff laughed his answer, "No, Mom. What's up with you?"

"Nothing, really."

"Something's wrong!"

"No, no. I just forgot to make a hair appointment, that's all. I used to go every Wednesday. Now, I go whenever I can and this week I forgot to call. They probably won't be able to fit me in."

Taking the tray from his mother, Cliff bent and placed a quick peck on her head. "I'm sorry, Mom."

"Whatever for?"

"You're carrying a huge burden."

"Cliff, you and Denny are not a burden. You're my family. Please don't worry about me. I forgot to make an appointment, that's all."

Taking the tray back from Cliff, Susan rattled on, "I'll just call later. Maybe I can get an appointment for tomorrow."

"Don't waste your money, Mom. You look beautiful to me. Skip your appointment this week."

Appointment!

Checking the kitchen clock, Susan silently willed her son to leave.

If you leave right now, Cliff, I'll have enough time to get Denny ready. Leave. Leave. **Please leave***.*

As though ushered out by her silent pleas, Cliff left, and Susan tried to calm herself.

8

The two women eased quietly into the upstairs bedroom just after 10:00. Careful not to disturb Denny, Dr. Malone positioned herself in such a way that she had an unobstructed view of her new patient. Focusing on Denny Jameson's eyes, Dr. Malone waited for the slightest movement, for the slightest indication that said she knew they were there. Receiving none, Dr. Malone turned her attention to the window that Denny peered through. A gentle rain tapped a tender tune on the partially fogged windowpane, but Denny seemed not to notice. Just as she seemed not to notice playful droplets of rain as they danced along the glass before scurrying from view.

Pulling a pad and pen from her pocket. Dr. Malone quickly made a note. **No eye movement.** Sure that she filled Denny's peripheral vision, she made another note. **Aware/unaware of my presence?** Dropping a leather-bound calendar onto the floor, Dr. Malone waited for the 'thud', then when Denny jumped, she made another note in her pad. **Responsive to sudden sounds.**

Moving toward the nightstand, Dr. Malone lifted a beautiful silver frame that held a darling picture of two blond curly-top cherubs. The boy, dressed in jeans and work boots, appeared to be about four or five years old. The girl, all dolled up in a white, eyelet sundress and hat, was considerably younger. Smiling through heavily cracked glass, the sweet faces of Denny Jameson's deceased children pulled Dr. Malone's heartstrings.

Finally eliciting a response, Dr. Malone watched as Denny turned her head toward her. Amazed by her patient's non-verbal response to the blatant invasion of privacy, Dr. Malone locked onto Denny's heavily hooded eyes. Could almost hear her silent command.

Put it down!

Feeling the intensity of Denny's long, cold, hard stare, Dr. Malone placed the picture frame back onto the nightstand, and made another note. **Communicating ... loud and clear!**

"That's it? Aren't you even going to say anything to her?"

"Mrs. Jameson, your daughter-in-law and I had plenty to say to one another."

"But neither of you spoke."

"Talking isn't the only form of communication."

"It's not?"

"No. Even though Denny and I didn't 'speak' in the traditional sense, we 'spoke'."

"What do you mean?"

"At first, I wasn't sure Denny was aware of her surroundings, let alone that we were even there. But, she knew."

"How do you know?"

"When I picked up the picture of her children, she stared me down. Challenged me. Made me uncomfortable. Ultimately, I put the picture back."

"That was communication?"

"Maybe not to you and me. But to Denny, it was communication. It may be the only kind she's comfortable with right now. In any event, her message was loud and clear. It's a good sign. Really."

Nestled back into bed, Denny closed her eyes. Sleep beckoned her, but she couldn't answer its call. Something was bothering her. Something kept her from her treasured respite.

Something is wrong. What? What's wrong?

Struggling to keep her fatigued eyes open, Denny searched her room. Finding the black velvet backing of the silver picture frame facing her bed, Denny silently cursed the mystery woman for touching her prized possession.

I told you to leave it alone. Now look, I can't see their faces.

Sliding her hand along the smooth wood of her night stand, Denny gently inched the frame toward her. When her eyes finally fell upon the shattered glass images of her precious children, her broken heart skipped a beat.

9

Denny had no idea what day it was, but she knew the routine.

Shower … bed … no visitor.

Shower … rocking chair … visitor.

Sitting in her rocking chair by the window that morning, Denny waited. While she waited, she prayed.

I hope she comes today. Please God, let her come.

Before long, Denny's prayer was answered. Quietly, gently, the mystery woman took her usual place across from Denny, leaning with her back pressed tightly against the far wall.

I wonder who she is.

"Denny, I'm Dr. Malone, Dr. Beth Malone. Your mother-in-law asked me to come see you. I'll be doing that every week until you're ready to come see me. Okay?"

You come see me … okay. I come see you … I don't think so.

"Denny, I'm a doctor. That's important for you to know. What's more important, is that I'm a therapist."

A therapist? I must really be in bad shape if Cliff agreed to therapy!

"Do you know what therapy is?"

When Denny nodded, Dr. Malone quickly jotted a note. **Patient responsive.**

"Have you ever had therapy before?"

No, but I needed it. I wanted it.

Denny's thoughts were conveyed by a slight shake of her head.

"Do you think you need therapy, Denny?"

Again, Denny nodded.

"Good, in order for therapy to work, the people involved need to work together. Do you think you're up to working with me?"

Denny nodded.

"Very well, then, I think we should get to know each other. Like I said my name is Beth Malone. You can call me Beth. Is it okay that I call you Denny?"

A nod.

"Okay Denny, now for some ground rules. Whatever you tell me, stays with me. If you choose to discuss our sessions with other people, that's fine, but no one ... NO ONE ... will hear what goes on in our sessions from me."

No one?

"Does that seem right to you, Denny?"

A silent nod said that she agreed and understood.

Beth moved toward Denny's side of the room. All the while, she kept eye contact with Denny.

"Would it be alright if I sat on the edge of the bed?"

Denny closed her eyes, then slowly opened them.

"Was that a yes, Denny?"

The eye movement was repeated.

"Good. Okay, let's begin."

"Denny, I'll ask you a series of questions. You can answer them any way you'd like. A nod or a shake of the head is fine. Even blinking is okay. Will that work?"

A blink.

"Denny. Do you know what day this is?"

Nothing.

"How about the date?"

Nothing.

"Season? Do you know what season it is?"

Spring.

Denny nodded.

"Good. Then you know it's spring?"

Denny nodded.

"Do you like spring, Denny?"

Nothing.

"Did you ever like spring?"

A tear slid down Denny's cheek.

"Are you sad, Denny?"

Looking past Beth, Denny locked her eyes on the silver picture frame. A deep, guttural moan shuddered through her, then she closed her eyes. After ten minutes of silence from Denny, Beth knew she had checked out for the day.

"Denny, are you getting tired?"

Nothing.

"You look tired. Why don't we stop for today. I'll come again next week. Okay?"

Nothing.

Susan had a cup of tea waiting for Dr. Malone.

"How's Denny?"

"She's resting. She worked very hard today."

"Worked hard? Does that mean she spoke?"

"Communicated, yes."

There's that word again; communicated. Maybe Cliff's right. Maybe therapy is just a bunch of hogwash!

"Mrs. Jameson, may I see Denny's prescriptions please?"

Handing Dr. Malone two bottles, Susan's caregiver persona took hold, "One's a mild sedative. The other's an anti-depressant."

"Yes, that's right."

"Are you thinking of changing the prescriptions? I mean that might make Cliff suspicious."

"No, no. Denny should continue the anti-depressant as prescribed by Dr. Valez. I just wanted the information for my records." After recording the date filled, prescription dosage, etc., Dr. Malone bid her farewell to Mrs. Jameson. Once outside, she glanced upward to see if

40

Denny was still sitting at her bedroom window. Sending a friendly wave toward the tiny figure, Beth waited for one in return. When she received none, she left.

Denny fell into a deep, coma-like sleep and slept most of the weekend. Try as he might, Cliff had trouble waking her for meals or for her medication. And showers, well they were definitely out of the question. Come Monday morning, both Denny and Cliff showed signs of their long weekend together.

When Susan returned Monday morning, she noticed the signs almost immediately. "Cliff, what's wrong?"

"Denny. The kids. Good God Mom, everything is wrong!"

Wanting, and needing to offer her son some comfort, Susan moved toward Cliff, only to have him move toward the back door.

"Mom, you never told me how difficult life would be."

Turning tear filled eyes toward the sun-drenched kitchen window, Susan reflected on what she could have possibly said to prepare her son for the horrors he was now living through.

Cliff, even if I somehow knew that any of this would happen, How Could I have prepared you? What words could I have said that would have mattered? What words might matter now?

Completely at a loss, Susan whispered the only words that seemed to make any sense, "I'm sorry, Cliff."

"Will it ever get any better, mom? Will Denny ever get any better?"

Tell him about the therapy ... Give him some hope.

"I don't know, Cliff. I hope she will. I pray that she will."

"But do you **believe** that she will?"

Tell him about the therapy.

"Yes. I do."

Shower ... back to bed. No visitor.
Shower ... back to bed. No visitor.
Shower ... back to bed. No visitor.
Shower ... rocking chair. **Visitor**.

When Beth entered Denny's room, she took her usual place against the far wall, on the other side of the windows that Denny sat before.

"Good morning, Denny."

Nothing.

"How are you feeling?"

Nothing.

"Have you been eating well?"

Nothing.

"Sleeping well?"

To that Denny shook her head.

"No?"

Beth quickly reviewed some of the notes she'd made after talking with Susan that morning. **Mother-in-law states patient spent entire weekend sleeping.**

"Are you sure you're not sleeping well, Denny?"

A nod.

"Do you know why?"

Nothing.

"Are you uncomfortable?"

Nothing.

"Frightened?"

A nod.

"Do you know what frightens you?"

Slowly, Denny's eyes turned toward the silver picture frame.

"Page and Preston frighten you?"

Giant tears answered Beth's question. As difficult as it was for Beth to do nothing, she forced herself to wait Denny's grief out, forced herself to watch where Denny's grief took her. After several minutes had passed, Beth quietly crossed the room and helped dry Denny's tear-stained cheeks and runny nose. Tentatively, she pressed Denny to continue.

"Denny, your trouble sleeping, is it because you're having dreams?"

Denny's nod was replaced by a slow, but determined blink.

"And your dreams are frightening you?"

Life without Page and Preston is frightening me.

"Are they Denny, are your dreams frightening you?"

When Denny blinked her response this time Beth knew they were done for the day. As she left Denny that morning, she left her with praise for her hard work, and a little homework, as well.

"Concentrate on your dreams, Denny. They might be trying to tell you something."

~~ 11 ~~

Susan spent the next weekend with Cliff and Denny. It was a good weekend. Cliff spent some time doing yard work, and Denny managed to get herself to the rocking chair unassisted. She managed a little homework too.

When Beth joined Denny that Thursday, she took her usual place against the wall. After giving Denny a moment to adjust to her presence, she addressed her client.

"I heard you've been sleeping better."

I thought you said you wouldn't talk about me.

The immediate change in Denny's body language sent Beth a message as loud and clearly as if Denny screamed her complaint from the rooftop.

"Denny, something is wrong. What is it?"

You figure it out.

Replaying what little conversation they'd had, Beth took a stab.

"Denny, remember when I told you that I wouldn't repeat anything we said during our sessions?"

Nothing.

"That's still the case. But it's important for me to get information about you from people who care about you. They're like eyes and ears for me. Do you understand that, Denny?"

Shifting back into her original position, Denny turned open, receptive eyes toward Beth.

"Good. May we begin then?"

A long slow blink let Beth know things were okay between them. Turning her attention away from Denny for a moment Beth reviewed several pages of her notes. By the time she focused on Denny again, she was crying.

"Denny, you're sad."

A nod.

"About Page and Preston?"

A nod.

"It's okay to be sad, Denny."

As though Beth had given the grief-stricken woman some sort of permission to share her pain Denny's floodgates burst. Deep, racking sobs violently shook the frail creature's body as though it were a rag doll being mauled by a ferocious animal. Remaining perfectly still, Beth watched as Denny rode her grief downward. It was a pitiful, painful sight to see. Unfortunately, it was also necessary.

Taking a generous supply of tissues with her, Beth helped Denny wipe her face and blow her nose. This simplest of gestures brought her great rewards.

"Thank you."

Unsure she heard what she thought she heard; Beth uttered a response anyway.

"You're welcome."

Dropping her head to her chest, Denny rode another current of tears before speaking again.

"Beth, I hurt so badly that sometimes I can't breathe. Sometimes I wish I wouldn't."

"Breathe?"

"Breathe. Feel."

"The breathing will take care of itself Denny, why don't we concentrate on the feelings. Okay?"

"Okay."

"Good. Denny, can you tell me what you're feeling?"

"Heart-stopping, bone-crushing pain, and an overwhelming sense of guilt."

Beth had made assumptions of who Denny was and what she would sound like. She based those assumptions partly on Denny's fragile state, and partly on Denny's waif-like appearance. Tiny and blonde, broken silver picture frame. Sweet, innocent, vulnerable. That's what Beth had assumed Denny would be like. Having heard her speak, Beth realized how very wrong she had been.

The Denny sitting before her was articulate, clear, precise. Fully aware of her emotions, and desperate to look at them, perhaps even work at them.

"Guilt. Can you tell me about the guilt?"

"I didn't pick Page and Pres up from school that last day. If I had, they would still be alive."

"Why didn't you pick them up?"

"I don't know."

"Don't know, or can't remember?"

"Don't know. Wait, that's not entirely true."

"No?"

"What I mean is, I **couldn't** pick them up. But I don't know why."

Fearing Denny might retreat into a world of silence, Beth ended their session with some well-deserved praise.

"Denny, you've done some amazing work here today. Next time we meet, maybe we can take a closer look at why you couldn't pick Page and Preston up. Okay?"

A troubling silence and stillness was Denny's only response. The same response she received when she waved up to Denny from the driveway a few minutes later.

~~ 12 ~~

Susan had no idea of the progress Denny had made that morning. She hadn't heard anything about it from Dr. Malone, nor from Denny who had gone back to her mute-like state the minute Beth had left. A state she would remain in until Beth's next visit.

"Good morning, Denny."

Nothing.

"I hear you have been getting up more often, staying up longer."

Nothing.

Beth made a few notes as she went along. They consisted of only two words. **Unresponsive. Why?**

"Denny, your mother-in-law didn't mention anything about our last session. About your speaking."

Nothing.

"Does she know you and I spoke during our last session?"

Nothing.

"Have you spoken to her or to your husband?"

"No."

"Okay. Would you like to speak to them?"

"No."

"Can you tell me why not?"

"What could I possibly say that would make a difference? Would saying I'm sorry change anything?"

"Are you sorry, Denny?"

"Of course!"

"Can you tell me what you're sorry about?"

Denny looked past Beth, locked her eyes on the silver picture frame. Accepting Denny's form of communication, Beth moved forward.

"You're sorry about Page and Preston?"

A silent nod, accompanied by giant tears, was Beth's only answer.

"About their deaths?"

Again, nothing but tears.

"Denny, you said last time that you felt guilty. Is that what you're feeling now?"

A nod.

"Because you didn't get the kids from school?"

A nod.

"But you also said that you didn't pick them up because you couldn't. Do you remember why you couldn't pick the kids up?"

"No. I just couldn't. It was just like all the other times when I couldn't pick them up. There were other times, you know. Lots of other times when I told the kids I'd be there, but ..."

"But, you weren't?"

51

"No."

"What did they do if you weren't there to get them?"

"They'd take the bus."

Floodgates burst. How could they not?

When Denny had composed herself, they gingerly trudged on.

"Denny, I'm going to recap what we've covered. I need you to bear with me, okay?"

"Okay."

"So far, you've remembered that you couldn't get the kids from school that day. That there were a lot of other times when you told the kids you'd pick them up, but you didn't."

A nod.

"And, when you didn't pick the kids up, they would take the bus home?"

A nod.

"Denny, what happened when they took the bus home?"

"What?"

"On the days when the kids took the bus home, what happened?"

"I don't know. I just couldn't pick them up."

"Denny, I don't want you to focus on why you couldn't pick Page and Preston up. I want you to focus on what happened when you didn't pick them up."

Needing to shut the world out, Denny clamped her eyes shut. Needing her client to work through this point, Beth waited, and waited. Then, she waited some more. After more than ten minutes had passed, she feared she had lost Denny for the day. The eternal optimist, Beth gave it one more try.

"Denny, what happened to Page and Preston the other times they took the bus."

"Nothing."

"That's right. Nothing happened. They made it home safely, didn't they?"

"Yes."

Not wanting to lose the opportunity, Beth continued.

"Denny, what happened with the bus was an accident. A tragic accident. But, it's not your fault. Denny, the accident didn't happen because you weren't there to get Page and Preston from school. It just happened. It was an accident. Can you see that?"

Overwhelmed by Beth's words, Denny surrendered to her pain, her grief, her guilt. As deep guttural moans filled the space between the two women, Beth knew that Denny would never be the same again. She also knew that she wouldn't be the same either.

~~ 13 ~~

As usual, Susan was waiting for Beth in the kitchen.

"How was the session?"

Exhausted from the rigor of her session with Denny, Beth gladly accepted a seat at the chair Susan offered her. "Actually, Mrs. Jameson, I'd like to talk with you about Denny's sessions."

"Really?"

"I'd like to double up on them."

"Double up?"

"Yes, add another hour, beginning next week."

Flipping through her calendar, Beth rattled on. "I could come Tuesdays from two to three, or if it's more convenient, I could extend our Thursday appointment by an hour. Come at nine instead of ten, and stay until eleven. Would that be better for you?"

"Another hour. Oh, I'm not sure."

"I think Denny would benefit from an additional session, more importantly, I think she'll tolerate more time nicely. She's ready."

"Ready? Really? There's been some progress then?"

"About the sessions. Which would you prefer, Mrs. Jameson, another day, or a longer session?"

Rubbing the back of her neck, Susan hemmed a little, hawed a little. "Oh, I'm not sure. I guess a longer session would be easier for me. You know Cliff still doesn't know about the therapy, and I'd like to keep it that way. At least until there is some progress to report."

Susan turned sheepish, questioning eyes toward Beth, "Is there any progress to report?"

Snapping her calendar closed, Beth moved to the back door, "Okay then, Thursday, nine to eleven. Perfect."

Denny watched from her bedroom window. *Where is she?*

Her eyes fixed on the driveway; Denny knew she hadn't missed Beth leaving. Knew Beth was still downstairs.

What's she doing? Talking to Susan? Telling her about our conversations?

Within moments, Denny caught a glimpse of Beth as she waved to her from the driveway. As usual, Denny did not return Beth's wave.

Denny was still by the window when Susan brought her lunch.

"You're still up. That's wonderful. Maybe you are making progress. I asked Dr. Malone, but she's a tight lipped one. Never says a thing."

Good. She shouldn't.

Relieved that Beth hadn't betrayed her, Denny sipped some chicken broth. It was warm and salty and it was delivered by the loving hand of her mother-in-law. Turning grateful eyes toward Susan, Denny silently implored Susan to notice.

Susan noticed. "Oh, Denny. I think you **are** making progress. I'm so glad I took Dr. Malone's advice."

Advice? What advice?

Leaning in toward her daughter-in-law, Susan whispered into Denny's ear. "Dr. Malone wants to double up on your appointments. Spend more time with you, beginning next week. I wasn't sure at first, but now I see that she **is** helping you. And that makes me very happy."

Susan, you're whispering. Why are you whispering?

"You know, Denny, Cliff doesn't know about your therapy."

*What! You're kidding, right? No, of course you aren't kidding. I should have known better. Cliff would **never** approve of therapy.*

Looking deeply into Susan's eyes again, Denny tried to express her gratitude.

Susan, you found Beth for me. Thank you. And, don't worry, Susan, I won't tell Cliff, I promise.

Grabbing a tissue, Susan gently dabbed at Denny's sweet face.

"I'm sorry, Denny. I've upset you. I didn't mean to upset you."

Over dinner that night, Susan told Cliff how much brighter Denny seemed. Still, she left out the part about therapy.

"Brighter?"

"Yes, she made eye contact with me, for just a moment, mind you, but during that moment I think she understood what I was saying. No, I'm sure of it. Denny knew what I was saying to her."

"Really? That's wonderful!" Cliff said as he left the dinner table and raced up to the second floor. Bursting into the bedroom, Cliff found Denny exactly as he'd left her that morning. Sleeping. Deflated, he rejoined his mother at the table.

"I don't know, Mom. I don't see any changes."

"Maybe you will over the weekend. Maybe you could spend some time with Denny during the day. She seems brighter during the days."

The weekend came. The weekend went. Cliff didn't see any brighter days. Denny didn't see the days at all.

She slept the entire weekend.

~~ 14 ~~

The following Thursday, Susan met Dr. Malone at the door.

"Dr. Malone, I'm so glad we decided to extend the sessions."

"Has something happened?"

"Last week after you left, I think Denny made eye contact with me. No, I know Denny made eye contact!"

"Good. That's very good."

Before Beth had finished her sentence, there was a noticeable change in Susan.

"Mrs. Jameson. Is something wrong?"

"Cliff didn't see any change in Denny. When I told him Denny seemed brighter, he was so excited. He raced to Denny's side, but by then, she was sleeping. She slept the entire weekend, so Cliff never did get a chance to spend time with her. I know if he had, he would have seen a difference. Maybe he would have seen that the situation isn't hopeless."

"Hopeless? No, no, Denny's situation isn't hopeless, Mrs. Jameson."

"Dr. Malone, you know that, and I know that, but Cliff, he definitely does not know that. And if there's anyone who needs to know there is reason for hope, it's Cliff."

"Your son; he still doesn't know about our therapy sessions?"

Susan shook her head.

"Maybe he should, Mrs. Jameson. Maybe you should reconsider and tell him."

"Tell him what?"

A startled Susan and Beth stared at the silhouetted figure filling the back door. Neither spoke.

Staring back, Cliff asked his question again, "Tell him what?"

Susan broke the silence, "Cliff, my goodness, you startled me. I can only imagine how Beth feels."

"Beth?"

"Yes, Beth"

Susan quickly made introductions. They were awkward, but more importantly, they were a down-right lie!

"Cliff, Beth is the niece of Mrs. Hawkins from the beauty salon, you've heard me mention her, haven't you?"

Susan waited for a response, when she received none, she rattled on some more.

"Anyway, Betty, Mrs. Hawkins, mentioned to Beth that I've been stopping in the beauty salon now that I'm back in town most of the time. Betty must have mentioned Denny, and her unfortunate situation to Beth because this sweet thing …"

Wrapping her arm around Beth's shoulder, Susan pulled her close before continuing, "This sweet thing, stopped by today to see if I needed anything. Wasn't that sweet, Cliff? A young woman like her taking time out of her busy schedule to stop by."

Desperate to free himself from the chattering, Cliff explained the reason he'd returned home. "I forgot my checkbook this morning. I need to stop at the cleaners for my uniform."

Pulling open the top drawer of a built-in desk, Susan grabbed Cliff's checkbook and handed it to him.

"You need your uniform? I haven't seen you in uniform since your last promotion."

"Yeah, I've got a paid detail this weekend. There's a dance over at the high school Saturday night. The school hires a few cops to stand around, keep an eye on things, bust up any fights. I signed up for the shift. It's easy money. Besides, I could use a change of pace."

Heading for the door, Cliff made eye contact one more time with Beth. "It was nice to meet you, Beth. Thanks for checking in on Mom. You're welcome anytime."

Denny watched from her window as Cliff headed toward his unmarked car. Little waves of fear danced along her fingers and toes as she wondered about the happenings downstairs.

If Cliff found out what Beth's doing here, he'll make Susan fire her. Maybe he already fired her.

Her eyes fixed on the driveway, Denny began a silent little prayer that she repeated over and over.

I hope he didn't find out why Beth's here. Please don't let Cliff find out why Beth's here. Please! I hope he didn't find out why Beth's here. Please don't let Cliff find out why Beth's here. Please!

On his way down the driveway, Cliff checked out Beth's car.

Midnight blue Volvo. Nice ride.

Like a bee to a flower, his mind was drawn to the image of Beth. His filthy mind was filled with the image of the tall, lovely woman.

Bet she's a nice ride, too.

~~ 15 ~~

As Beth climbed the stairs, she thought about the scene in the kitchen. It didn't sit well with her, and she told herself so. In fact, she found herself being her own therapist.

Beth. You're uncomfortable. What's making you so uncomfortable?

Being dishonest.

Why are you being dishonest?

Because it's the only way I can help Denny.

So, you agreed to become part of a situation that's built around dishonesty?

Yes.

To help Denny?

Yes.

Okay, helping Denny's a good thing … sometimes good things cost. What's the cost of helping Denny?

Honesty.

Can you help Denny if you're honest.

No.

Why not?

Because of Denny's husband.

What about Denny's husband?

I'm not sure, but he makes me uncomfortable.

So, it isn't dishonesty that makes you uncomfortable after all?

No.

It's Denny's husband that makes you uncomfortable?

Yes.

Denny was eager to get things going that morning. She started speaking the second Beth entered her room.

"Susan told me Cliff doesn't know that you're seeing me."

"That's right."

"But he just left."

"Yes."

"He met you?"

"Yes."

"Who did he think you were?"

"A visitor of Susan's."

Pleased that Susan and Beth had pulled a fast one on Cliff, Denny moved on.

"I've been thinking about that last day."

Knowing that Denny's reference to 'that last day' was her way of identifying Page and Preston's last day, Beth offered a moment of silent reflection for Denny's sake. When Denny continued, Beth realized that she meant business.

"Or maybe I was dreaming about that last day. Anyway, it really bothers me that I didn't pick up Page and Pres.

"Because of what happened?"

"Yes, of course, but …"

"Go on, Denny."

"I **promised** to pick them up that day. But, I didn't. Why?"

"So, it's the 'why' that's bothering you?"

A nod.

"Okay, let's figure out why you didn't pick up Page and Preston."

A nod.

"Tell me about that day. Tell me in as much detail as you can."

Instinctively, Denny closed her eyes and breathed deeply.

"It started like any other day. The alarm went off, I grabbed a quick shower, woke the kids, then headed downstairs to make their breakfast."

"How did you feel that morning?"

Denny's eyes were still closed.

"I had a headache."

"Did you take anything for it?"

"No."

"Okay, you get the kids their breakfast. Then what?"

"I packed their lunches and backpacks, then I quizzed Pres with his spelling words."

Beth expected Denny to lose her composure. Denny surprised her when she pushed through the pain and moved on. She seemed determined, for the first time, to remember the day.

"It was raining that morning, so traffic was heavier than usual. Page was afraid we'd be late, but we weren't. We pulled into the school's driveway a few minutes before the last bell. Pres hopped out of the van, sprinted into the school with a breezy wave over his shoulder.

"Page, on the other hand, dawdled for a bit. I could tell something was on her mind. Could tell she wanted to say something."

"Did she?"

"She asked me to pinky swear that I'd pick her up. I had every intention of picking them up that day, so I pinky swore."

Through heartbreaking sobs, Denny whispered the rest, "I broke the last promise I made to my daughter, and I didn't kiss my son goodbye."

Beth filled several pages with notes, ending them with a question.

Grief, sadness, guilt. Patient works at the fringes of these emotions, but seems to ignore their full range in order to pursue an answer to a question she's fixated on. That question: Why couldn't she pick her children up from school 'that day'?

He drove past his house a little before eleven, and found that the blue Volvo was still there. He wanted to go back in. He wanted to get to know Beth a little better.

Beth.

He'd always loved that name.

Beth.

He let his mind wander to the beauty inside his home.

Her name suits her. Simple. Natural. Elegant. That's not to imply that simple means plain, or natural means ugly, or elegant means snooty. On the contrary. Beth was beautiful.

Simply beautiful. Naturally beautiful. Elegantly beautiful. Beth.

God, how he loved that name! Sitting all alone in his unmarked car, Cliff repeated it over and over and over, and each time he said it, it sounded the same.

Like a whisper. A sexual whisper. Beth.

When she was finished with her session, Beth joined Mrs. Jameson at the kitchen table.

"Mrs. Jameson, do you have a moment?"

"Of course, but please, call me Susan."

"Thank you. Susan, I have a question about Denny's name. It's an unusual name for a woman."

"Yes, it is."

"Is it a nickname, or perhaps a family name?"

"Denny was named after her father. From what I understand, her parents were sixteen when Denny was conceived. Soon after learning of the pregnancy, the father skipped town. The mother, sure he'd return one day, wanted their child to share his name. So, she named her daughter Denny. As it turned out, Denny ended up sharing her name with a man she's never met. What I've been told is that Denny's father never returned. Can't say I blame him."

"Why's that?"

"Denny and her mother lived in a pitiful little shack over in Bakersville. We went by there once; it broke my heart thinking anyone lived in that dreadful place. Let alone someone my son was interested in. I remember the first time Cliff brought Denny home for dinner. She was this little bit of a thing, didn't look to be more than twelve. But, when she opened her mouth, she showed her maturity. She was wise beyond her years. Proud. Dignified. Not a silly, foolish bone in her body. She was hard-working through and through, put her everything into whatever she did. School. Marriage. Motherhood."

"I can tell you're very fond of your daughter-in-law. She is lucky to have you."

"Oh yes. Well ..."

The unfinished sentence told Beth there was more. After studying Susan for a moment, she knew there was more.

She's troubled by something.

"Susan, I want you to know that whatever you share with me, stays between you and me. So, if there's something that might help Denny, I'd appreciate knowing it."

"Dr. Malone. I love Denny. Always have, always will. Having said that, I can't say that I understand her behavior over the past few months. But I try not to judge. Really, I do."

"Her behavior? Since the accident?"

"No, no. Denny's behavior after the accident seems quite normal to me. She's a mother who lost her children in a freak accident. She's grieving. Believe you me, I understand what a powerful force grief is. It eats you alive, then spits you out when it's through with you. So,

68

I ask you, who's to say if there is a right way or a wrong way to handle the pain of grief? Not me.

"However, that's not to say that I think Denny went into that tragedy a whole person, because that's just not the case. No, something was different with Denny long before the accident. Maybe that something is making it more difficult for her to handle her pain now."

"Do you have any idea what was wrong?"

"Denny didn't even know."

"But she **knew** something was wrong?"

"We all did."

"All?"

"Cliff, Denny, me, the kids."

"Page and Preston noticed something?"

Susan nodded.

Beth was surprised by this and wanted to clarify. "Page and Preston knew something was wrong with their mother?"

"Page mostly. Though she never used the word 'wrong'."

"What word did she use?"

"Different. Page said Denny was different."

~~ 17 ~~

"Denny was different. Can you explain it to me?"

"Dr. Malone, I live about forty minutes from here, so I don't have a full picture of what was going on. But from what Page said, Denny seemed preoccupied. My word, not Page's.

"And forgetful, too. From what I understand, Denny would tell the kids she'd pick them up from school, then never show. Or from a friend's house, and again, she'd forget to pick them up, or arrive really late. She never had, or offered an explanation.

"Soon Denny began missing school functions, too. I remember how upset Page was when her mother missed a noontime play she was in. Because Denny had promised Page she'd be there, Page expected her. And because Denny was one of those mothers who never missed a school event, the principal expected her and even delayed the start of the production for her. When Denny didn't show, the principal called Cliff to make sure she was alright."

"Was she? Alright?"

"I guess that depends on what 'alright' means. Physically, I guess she was fine, but something was wrong somewhere. The hardest part for Page and Preston was that Denny never had an explanation for her behavior. I wish she had. It would have meant so much to the kids."

Pulling a tissue from her pocket, Susan gently collected her tears before continuing. "Like I said before, I wasn't always around when Denny blanked out — or had a spell — or whatever you want to call it. But when I was, I could tell how disturbed Denny was. Disturbed and confused."

"Susan, does Denny have any medical conditions?"

"No, not that I'm aware of."

"Insomnia? Narcolepsy? Alcoholism?"

"No."

"How about drugs? Any history of drug abuse?"

"No."

"Mental illness?"

"No, no. Until six months or so ago, Denny was perfectly normal. A wonderful wife, mother, daughter-in-law."

"Susan, what about Denny's friends? Did they notice a change in her as well?"

"Friends? I can't say Denny had any close friends. Acquaintances, plenty. But in all the years I've known her, I don't recall her mentioning anyone special."

"Never? How about when you first met her?"

"If you'd seen where Denny lived Dr. Malone, you'd understand. It wasn't exactly the type of home you'd want to invite company to. If Denny was a bit of a loner, it probably has to do with where she came from."

Cliff found Denny sitting by the window that evening, so he tested her.

"Did you have a nice visit today?"

Nothing.

"Gee, maybe Mom didn't bring her friend up to see you. Did she, Denny? Did Beth come see you?"

Again, nothing.

"It would be okay if Beth came to see you, Denny. Might even do you some good to spend some time with Beth."

Cliff moved close to Denny. Watched her face for any sign that she'd heard him. Understood him.

Denny made sure he received nothing for his efforts.

Cliff knew he had an audience as he headed for his extra pay job that Saturday night. For a moment he thought about waving to Denny like he used to when he left. Then he thought … *What the hell for?*

~~ 18 ~~

He had watched the young couple all night, so when they snuck from the high school gymnasium, he knew where they were headed. He waited a few moments, gave them enough of a head start, then he followed them.

The young lovers didn't have a clue he'd followed them — that he watched them as they hopped into Daddy's car. They had no clue he watched the boy lift the girl's pink fuzzy sweater over her head and he watched as he hungrily kissed her mouth, neck, breasts.

He waited for them to get into it, really into it, then he moved silently through the parking lot toward their car. He wanted to watch. He needed to watch. Fortunately for him, the lovers were too busy to notice him. Taking his position near the 'sex mobile', he leaned against a beat-up Chevy Nova and lit a butt. Never taking his eyes off the young couple, he decided then and there that he liked what he saw. Really liked it.

His view unobstructed, he watched as fuzzy pink sweater girl straddled her date's eager lap.

Then he watched as the young lovers moved in unison.

This isn't a first for these two.

That excited him. The girl excited him.

From his vantage point, he had a perfect view of the girl, her hair, her shoulders, her breasts. He stared at her breasts. Soft, filtered light fell across them as they rose and fell in concert with her movements.

Nice tits. Firm, not too big, but certainly more than a mouthful.

Standing alone in the parking lot, he realized he was getting excited. Very excited. The familiar strain of his pants called out to him. He wanted to be part of the excitement. He needed to be part of it.

All too quickly, he heard a moan, a deep, stuttering moan, followed by several quick gasps for air. When silence filled the space where lust once lived, the young stud collapsed against the bucket seat where he remained — motionless.

The girl, well she kept riding her young man. Hoping. Needing. Wanting. All the while riding. Riding. Riding.

Amateurs.

Fuzzy pink sweater girl was riding her date when he made his move.

With his back to the young couple, he tapped on the passenger window with his nightstick.

"The party's inside kids. Let's move it along."

As the young lovers hurried into their clothes, he heard fuzzy pink sweater girl giggle. She had a deep, throaty giggle, one that sent flashes of excitement through him. Excitement she had missed out on with her young lover.

He thought of being with the fuzzy pink sweater girl; of what he would have done to her — with her. How he'd have pleased her, and he **would** have pleased her!

Yes, if you'd been with me baby, you would have done more than giggle.

He slowed his pace when he saw **her** standing by the flagpole. After all, she was the real reason he'd taken the extra pay job at the high school, the real reason he had slipped out to the parking lot, the real reason for so many things in his life.

Leaning against the solid brick building, he waited until fuzzy pink sweater girl and her lucky boyfriend went back inside. Then he motioned for **her** to join him.

She did.

Sliding his arm around her waist, he pulled her close. Playfully licking her lips, he waited until she opened her mouth to him then slipped his tongue into her mouth. Her sweet, pepperminty mouth.

After one long kiss, he pulled away. Gasping for air, she pulled his head forward, only to have him pull away again. Grabbing her hand, he pulled her through the parking lot toward the 'sex mobile'.

"Quick. Get in."

"Whose car is this?"

"Belongs to a friend. Get in."

Pulling her onto his lap, he busied himself with her top and bra, while she greedily worked at his fly. Ignoring her lips and shoulders, he headed immediately for her breasts. Pulling an eager nipple into his mouth, he sucked, licked, and bit until she moaned.

Reaching down between her legs, he groped until he found what he was searching for. An invitation. A soft, wet invitation. Answering the RSVP, he slid himself into her. All the way into her. Again, soft, pleading moans filled the still night around them.

Taking hold of her hips, he directed her. Lifted her, lowered her, lifted and lowered, again and again. When he felt her release, he pushed himself as far into her as he could so that she would know that he was hers and she was his.

Spent, she moved off him and into the empty bucket seat. Then, just like fuzzy pink sweater girl, she giggled.

"Your friend. What if he finds out about this?"

"He'll think I'm crazy."

"You are crazy."

He pulled her close. "About you."

"Yeah?"

"Yeah."

He knew what was coming next. He didn't try to stop it. After all, he owed her.

"Then why don't you come around."

He laughed. "I believe I just did."

"Funny. No really Cliff, I miss you."

"I know, I miss you too. But..."

"But, Denny still needs you, right?"

He nodded.

She turned away.

Inching closer, he pulled her near, planted whisper soft kisses across her cheek.

"Come on, baby. Be patient. Just a little longer, please."

"How much longer?"

"A month, maybe. I really don't know."

"Really?"

"Really. Soon baby."

They separated at the gymnasium door.

Cliff resumed his role as rent-a-cop, and she resumed hers as high school principal.

~~ 19 ~~

Denny didn't hear Cliff return that evening.

She didn't hear, or see much of anything for several days.

That Thursday, only a handful of minutes separated Cliff's departure and Beth's arrival. Both Susan and Denny found that too close for comfort.

After her discussion with Susan the previous week, Beth came armed to take Denny in new directions. She hoped Denny would follow her, as she addressed her from across the room.

"Good morning, Denny. How are you?"

Nothing.

"You should be well rested. I hear you slept quite a bit since Saturday."

Nothing.

"Has your sleeping become more peaceful?"

"No."

"Are you still dreaming?"

"Yes."

"About?"

"I can't remember."

"But you remember that your dreams bother you?"

"Yes."

"Denny, would it be alright if we talk about the dreams another time? Maybe spend our time today talking about you? I don't know much about you, Denny, and I'd like to."

Nothing.

"Denny, can you tell me who Denny Jameson is?"

Silence.

I'm a mother — no, not anymore. Okay, I'm a wife — wait, I'm not sure I'm that anymore either. A daughter-in-law, yes, I'm Susan's daughter-in-law — maybe not for long though.

Denny rolled the titles over and over before answering.

"I'm nobody."

Beth jotted some notes before continuing.

"Denny, do you have any hobbies?"

Silence.

I'm a soccer mom — except in our case it's baseball for Pres and softball for Page — and since I'm no longer a mom, I guess I no longer have any hobbies.

"No, no hobbies."

"Do you work?"

Ha! The age-old question, do stay-at-home moms work? I work taking care of my children — my family — and since I no longer have a family, I guess I no longer work.

"No, I don't work."

"Tell me about Cliff."

"What about him?"

"How you two met, how long you've been married, that sort of thing."

"We met at a high school football game. After the game, actually. I went to Bakersville High, Cliff went to Parker Academy. Bakersville hosted Parker during the regional playoffs. It was a big deal. Bakersville had never gone to regionals. Anyway, the night of the big game, every student who showed up was given something to do. Organize a pep rally, scavenger for a bonfire, work the ticket booth, things like that. I was put in charge of the after-game hot chocolate.

"As students and faculty of Parker Academy boarded the buses, I offered them cups of steaming hot chocolate. I'd set up a table in the parking lot with cups, napkins, and a huge push button thermos. It was freezing out, so I was kept busy. Practically every Parker Academy student took a cup of hot chocolate, if only to toss them out the bus windows. Anyway, one of the cups landed at my feet, hot chocolate splashed all over my slacks. My only decent pair of beige wool slacks.

"Cliff was heading to the bus at the time. He stopped and apologized for his teammate's behavior. About a week later I was called to the principal's office. He handed me an envelope. It contained ten dollars, and a note."

"What did it say."

"Hope this covers the cost of your dry cleaning. Cliff."

"How did he know who to send the money to?"

"I asked the principal the same thing. He didn't know. Eventually, I asked Cliff. His answer was simply that he knew everything. And, he did. He knew how to find out who I was, knew I wasn't seeing anyone. By the time I got up enough nerve to tell him where I came from, he confessed he already knew that, too.

"Back then, I thought his knowing everything was romantic, maybe even heroic. It gave him a larger-than-life quality. Like a superhero. I'd never had a superhero in my life, or any man for that matter. In no time at all, Cliff made up for that."

Beth jotted a few notes as she played Denny's words over in her head.

*Cliff knows **everything**!*

Cliff knew he'd find the blue Volvo outside his home that Thursday morning. He didn't know how he knew, but he knew. He always knew — everything.

~~ 20 ~~

Cliff waited to see if his mother mentioned Beth's visit that day.

She didn't.

Later that evening, Cliff tested Denny about Beth's visit.

"How was your day, Denny? Anything exciting happen? Any visitors stop by?"

He knows. Just like he's always said, he knows everything.

Terrified, Denny remained perfectly still, offered Cliff nothing but silence.

Don't move. Don't even blink. He's watching. Waiting.

Cliff spent over an hour with Denny, asking questions, watching for any sign that she was aware of his questions, that she might be hiding something.

Denny gave Cliff nothing in return for his efforts.

By the time Cliff got Denny into bed that evening, she was exhausted, too exhausted to resist the tiny green pill Cliff slipped into her mouth.

Green pill? I thought my pills were white or purple.

Denny swallowed the tiny green pill. She had no choice.

Weeks earlier, Cliff had taken up residence in the upstairs guest room, leaving the master bedroom to Denny. The move had been his mother's suggestion, one he resisted at first, but after a few nights of sound sleep even he had to admit the sleeping arrangements made sense.

"Besides," his mother had said, "Denny needs her space."

Cliff gave Denny her space then, but he had no intention of giving her space on this night. No, this night he and Denny would be together. He would have her body, mind, and soul, if he chose. He would see to that. It was a sure thing.

Shortly after Cliff gave Denny the tiny green pill, he slid into bed next to her and waited. He didn't have to wait very long.

Almost immediately, Denny's body tossed, turned, and twitched in the bed next to Cliff. Soon, tiny beads of sweat broke out across her forehead, neck, and chest. Close to hysteria, then he pushed the bed covers aside as she struggled to undo the buttons on her nightgown.

Thrilled with the show, Cliff watched as a frenzied Denny freed herself from her nightgown. A trail of soft dew glistened invitingly over his wife's smooth, silky body. Running the back of his hand along Denny's cheek, Cliff followed the outline of her chin before dropping his hand on to his wife's chest' A lusty heat welcomed him. Beckoned him. Answering their call, Cliff slid his hand toward Denny's breasts and playfully pulled a nipple. As expected, it responded.

No denying the familiar strain across his pants, Cliff allowed his desire to mount, almost to a fevered pitch. He wanted her, thought about having his way with her, but angrily he resisted the temptation. He had a plan for that night, so he forced himself to follow the plan. After all, there were more important things for him to do that evening. More important than fucking Denny. Way more important. Yes, fucking Denny would just have to wait.

After dressing Denny again and buttoning her top, Cliff pulled the covers up over her, then tuck them tightly around her. Almost mummifying her in the process. Cliff waited for the show to continue.

Before long the memories of that last day came flooding back, locking her in a prison of pain.

"Page, Preston, come on. School's not going to wait for you two, so come on. Breakfast is waiting. Hey Pres, make sure you bring your spelling words with you, we'll go over them while you eat."

Page bounced into the kitchen; her face practically hidden behind a halo of golden curls.

"Honey have your breakfast. Mommy will do your hair while you eat."

"Not in a ponytail, okay? Pigtails, I want pigtails today."

When Preston made his presence known, it was at his sister's expense. "You've already got one pig's tail, why would you want two more?"

"Mom! Tell him to stop."

"You tell him."

"Knock it off, butthead."

"Page Susan Jameson, that's enough. Butthead? Where did you hear such a thing?"

"On the bus."

"Well, no bus today. I'm picking you up."

Page was thrilled with this news. Preston was not.

"Aw come on, Mom. The bus is fun. We love taking the bus."

"No we don't, butthead."

"Page! Stop that."

Page ignored her mother's warning. She had more important things on her mind. "Mom, are you really going to pick us up? I mean really?"

Denny knew what Page meant by the 'really' so she tried to calm her daughter's fears.

"Yes honey, I'll be there to get you."

Holding out her tiny hand, Page offered her mother her pinky and tentatively asked, "Pinky swear?"

Wrapping her hooked pinky around Page's, they pumped their hands a couple of times, as Denny recited her solemn vow.

"Pinky swear."

~~ 21 ~~

Pres hopped from the van almost before it came to a stop. Denny honked her horn and waved for him to return, but it was Preston's turn to ignore her. With only an obligatory wave her way, Preston kept going up the Steep concrete stairs.

Turning her attention to Page, Denny watched through the rear-view mirror as Page gathered her things. Taking her sweet time as she packed checked unpacked then packed her things away, Denny waited patiently for her daughter to ready herself. Not her things — herself.

Her eyes locked on Page, Denny noticed the timid glances being sent her way. It was obvious that Page had something on her mind, had something she wanted to say, but Denny hated broaching tender subjects right before sending her little one off for the day. So, she waited for Page to decide whether they would have a discussion about what was bothering her. Receiving only stolen glances and silence from the backseat, Denny offered Page a lifeline.

"Honey, I'll be here after school. No bus for you today. Okay?"

With that, Page wrapped her arms around Denny's neck and planted a loud, wet kiss on her cheek.

"Okay."

"Then off you go, Page. Have a great day. I love you!"

"Love you, too."

"Love you, three."

"Love you, four."

"Love you more."

It was the same thing every morning. It was their dance.

Cliff watched as a tormented Denny tossed and turned beside him. Listened as Denny called Page and Preston for breakfast. As she admonished Page for calling Preston a butthead. As she pinky swore that she would pick them up from school that day. It wasn't until he heard Denny recite the 'I Love You' poem she always shared with Page, that he showed any emotion.

Leaving Denny's bed, he picked up the broken silver frame from the nightstand, looked into the eyes of his children, and sobbed, "Why did you leave me?"

Off in a drug-induced oblivion, Denny surrendered to the memories of that last day. Eventually her memories brought her to her bedroom and to the feelings she had as she struggled to get off her bed. Almost immediately, anxiety danced along every fiber of her being and when the full extent of her memories hit her, they hit her hard!

Though her words were often slurred, Cliff had no trouble understanding what his wife murmured over and over.

"Last day. Their last day. Page and Pres don't get on the bus. Please. I need to get up. Please, don't get on the bus!"

Helplessly, hopelessly, Denny willed herself to stop remembering, but she couldn't. The memories had a firm hold on her. A firm hold of her mind, as well as her heart. A heart that pounded wildly in her chest, right before breaking into a million tiny pieces. Unable to free herself from the death-like dream, Denny played that final afternoon one last time.

Time. What time is it? One-twenty. Call the school. Tell them to have Page and Preston wait. Tell them not to take the bus. I'll be there. I promised. Something's wrong. I need help! What's wrong with me?

Screaming for her children, she slipped from her nightmare into a coma-like state. Horrified, Cliff watch as his wife's body lost all sense of life. Finding a weak pulse, Cliff checked Denny's respiration and reflexes, checking her eyes. Eyes that stared blankly up at him. Eyes that said his wife was alive, barely it seemed, but still she was alive.

Cliff stayed by Denny's side that night. He prayed that night, too. But as usual, his prayers were for himself. "Don't let her die. Please, don't let her die. There will be an investigation. They'll find out about the drugs." Gently shaking Denny's shoulders, Cliff begged her to regain consciousness. "Come on. Wake up. Don't you fucking die on me you bitch. Not now. It's almost over. I'm almost free. Come on. Wake up!"

Denny didn't wake up. Not that night, or for many more nights to come.

~~ 22 ~~

Susan met Beth on the driveway that following Thursday. It was immediately apparent that something was wrong. Terribly wrong.

"Susan, what is it?"

"It's Denny."

"Has something happened?"

Stealing a quick glance toward Denny's window, and finding it empty, Beth asked her question again. "Has something happened? Susan, where is Denny?"

Following Susan into the house, Beth raced up the stairs to Denny's room. Finding an almost lifeless form on the bed, Beth shouted her concern at Susan, "What happened to her?"

"I don't know."

"How long has she been like this?"

"Almost since your last visit."

Beth quickly replayed the events of their last visit.

It was a good visit. Productive. Too productive?

"Susan, why didn't you call me and tell me about Denny's condition?"

Beth thought she heard Susan say something about Cliff before firing another round of questions.

"Has she been up? Eaten? Taken her medication?"

Beth watched as Susan silently replied no with a quick shake of her head.

"Susan. Get on the other side. Lift her. Let's see if we can get her to sit up."

"In the chair?"

"No, lets prop her up against the headboard."

The women worked feverously, pushing, pulling, tugging, and tucking. All the while, Denny remained in some sort of catatonic state. Inside, however, she pleaded with them for help.

Cliff gave me a green pill. It knocked me out. Made me have horrible dreams. Then, it sent me into a deep, deep sleep. But, I'm not sleeping anymore. Maybe it looks like it to you, but I'm awake in here. Alive. Please help me. Beth, Susan, help me. Don't let him give me any more of those pills. Please!

Once Denny was comfortably propped up, Beth checked her from top to bottom. First, she took Denny's pulse, checked her reflexes, then her sensitivity to stimulation and pain. When she was finished with the cursory exam, she assessed Denny's level of mental capacity and made her customary notes.

Patient shows classic signs of catatonia. She's withdrawn, numb, has a stunned, but otherwise emotionless expression on her face, regardless of stimulation or pain I inflict.

Extremely concerned with Denny's condition, Beth busied herself with her care. First, she massaged Denny's legs, then her arms, all the while hoping for, searching for, a response in Denny's rigid muscles. Unfortunately, she found none. Still, Beth continued along Denny's shoulders, hands, and fingers.

Susan watched Beth work with Denny, found her touch gentle yet determined. It was obvious Beth was on a mission, and that mission, Susan decided, was to help Denny. Silently, Susan prayed that Beth could help her daughter-in-law.

The sudden sound of a car door interrupted Susan's prayer. Peeking from Denny's window, Susan watched as Cliff made his way up the driveway.

"Beth, its Cliff. Come on, we've got to get downstairs. Quick, come on."

"No, Susan, I'm staying here. You go if you want to, but I'm staying with Denny."

"You can't! What will I tell Cliff."

"I don't care what you tell him."

"Beth, Cliff will be very upset. Please. I'm not sure what he'll do if he finds out I went behind his back. Please, for Denny's sake, come on."

Reluctantly, Beth followed Susan downstairs. They met Cliff at the bottom step.

"There you are, Mom."

Kissing his mother's cheek, Cliff then addressed Beth.

"Well, what brings you around here, Beth?"

Susan answered, "She came to see Denny."

"Really? Why?"

Without missing a beat, Susan fed Cliff another set of lies.

"Beth offered to give Denny a massage."

"A massage?"

"To try to help keep Denny's muscles toned."

"Really? Are you a professional? Masseuse that is?"

"No, it's just a hobby."

"Interesting hobby."

The three of them shared a laugh in the tiny space at the bottom of the stairs. A very nervous laugh. All the while, Cliff eyed his mother. Looked at her as he'd looked at hundreds of suspects over the years. Saw on her what he often saw on them. Guilt.

Something's up. She's lying. They're lying. Why?

"So, Mom, how's Denny?"

"About the same, dear."

"Even after the massage?"

"Beth hasn't started yet. She was just about to when we heard you pull up."

"Oh well, don't let me keep you. I was in the neighborhood and just stopped in to grab another cup of coffee. I didn't mean to interrupt anything."

Then with a smile for the visitor, "It was nice seeing you again, Beth."

Cliff silently watched as the women climbed back up the stairs. Well, he watched Beth that is.

When Cliff climbed into his unmarked car a few minutes later, he felt the familiar strain across his pants. He was hard. Very hard. Closing his eyes, Cliff went with the feelings the beauty inside his home stirred. Before long, images of Beth massaging him flooded his brain as her name escaped his lips.

"Beth. Beth. Beth."

The way he said her name made it sound like a whisper.

A sexual whisper.

23

Right after lunch, Cliff ran the midnight blue Volvo's license plate. What he learned about the owner of the Volvo didn't please him.

"Hmm. Car is registered to Philip Malone."

Husband? Father? Brother? Friend?

Cliff thought back to his mother's introduction.

"Cliff, this is Beth."

Just Beth. No last name. Somehow, Cliff thought he'd heard a last name. He ran the rest of his mother's conversation about Beth through his head. *"Beth is the niece of Mrs. Hawkins from the beauty salon, you've heard me mention her, haven't you? Anyway, Betty, Mrs. Hawkins, mentioned to Beth that I've been stopping by the salon now that I'm in town. She even mentioned Denny and her unfortunate situation to Beth. Anyway, this sweet thing stopped by today to see if I needed anything. Wasn't that sweet, Cliff? A young woman like her taking time out of her busy schedule to visit me."*

Hawkins. In all that rambling, Cliff found that he had heard a last name. Still, he wasn't sure if it was Beth's last name. Still, he wasn't sure what her last name was.

Before heading home that evening, Cliff drove past the address listed on the Volvo's registration. 147 Hummingbird Lane. He knew the address was in an upscale section of town. Still, he was surprised by how 'upscale' it turned out to be.

147 Hummingbird Lane held a stately brick house situated nicely on a corner lot, flanked on three sides by bright pink Rhododendron bushes eager to bloom. Neighbors' homes were obscured by thick Laurel and Holly bushes that lent a very woodsy feel to the place.

Nice digs. Really nice digs.

Driving past her house, Cliff circled up around the block and came down a side street that offered a perfect view of the back of the house. The incredibly huge house. Cliff found that 147 Hummingbird Lane had three floors, two chimneys, and wall-to-wall windows that overlooked a magnificent yard and the circle driveway flanked on both sides by a gorgeous rock garden.

Scanning the empty driveway, Cliff's eye came to an abrupt halt on a small brick building set off to one side of the yard. The building was very similar in design to the main house, complete with wall-to-wall windows and a wrap-around porch.

Easing his car to the curb, Cliff kept his eyes trained on the small brick structure. Wondered the entire time what it could be.

It's too nice for a shed. Sheds don't usually have brick inlaid walkways leading to them. No, too nice. Way too nice.

He thought about Beth for a moment. About her 'hobby'.

Maybe she is a masseuse, and maybe she works out of that building. Maybe Philip Malone is her lover. Poor guy probably spends all day working so he can keep her living in the lap of luxury. And how does she repay him? She spends her days in that little building, running her hands over naked people, that's how.

The idea of his Beth running her hands over naked people thrilled him and disgusted him at the same time. Still, there was no escaping his thoughts — no escaping how hungry those thoughts made him. Hungry for the new object of his desire, Beth. He wanted her. Right then, right there. Sealing Beth's fate, Cliff decided that he would have his sweet Beth. When he wanted. How he wanted.

Not today, my sweet, sweet Beth. But soon. Very soon.

Cliff took one more look around Beth's property before heading out onto Hummingbird and toward Pleasant Street.

Incredibly preoccupied by Denny's state of health, Beth didn't notice the unmarked police car pass her as she turned off Pleasant Street onto Hummingbird Lane.

24

Cliff didn't bring any green pills to Denny that weekend. Only white oval ones, and shiny purple ones. Still, Denny knew she was being given the green ones too.

They're probably in the soup Susan's feeding me right now. Susan! Please stop! Check the soup, or the tea. Cliff's drugging me. I need your help. Please.

Susan spent the entire weekend with Cliff and Denny, and while there was no change in Denny, Susan noticed a definite change in Cliff.

"Is something wrong, Cliff?"

"You're kidding, right?"

"Is it Denny? Don't worry. I'm sure her current state is only a minor setback."

Angrily, Cliff stared at his mother. "A setback? Seriously? That implies that Denny's made progress and somehow that progress slipped away. There has been no setback Mom, because there's been no progress in the first place."

Susan disagreed. There had been progress. But, not wanting to risk Cliff finding out about Denny's therapy, Susan kept quiet. Very quiet.

By Saturday evening, Cliff wished he had sent his mother home for the weekend. But, he didn't. He couldn't. He had plans this weekend, and those plans included Susan.

Cliff spent all day Sunday locked in his study. Packing. Planning. Fantasizing. He liked his fantasies best, because they were about Beth. Only Beth. Closing his eyes, Cliff locked onto the image of Beth as she moved down the flight of stairs toward him. He studied her movements as she glided toward him, found them to be graceful, elegant. Very much like a ballerina.

Held prisoner by the image of Beth's body, Cliff waited as his fantasy took wings. A fantasy that had Beth, the dancer, dressed in skimpy pink leotard and tights, stretching before a dancer's barre. Slowly, Cliff studied her long muscled legs, narrow hips, and flat, taut abdomen. Her image set in his mind, he moved his gaze upward over her midriff, stopping when hard, pointed nipples greeted him, beckoned him through the tightly stretched leotard. As though he had a choice, he focused on Beth's delicate, perfectly round, firm breasts that barely moved as she performed her exercises. Forcing himself to keep going, Cliff's fantasy filled his mind. Moving up past Beth's long sleek neck, to her finely chiseled face that held small, angular features. Her long, stick straight corn silk blonde hair was pulled into a high ponytail, held in place with a pink satin ribbon. Tiny pearl studs graced each ear.

Captured by the beauty conjured in his mind's eye, Cliff welcomed the familiar strain that bound him tightly in his jeans. Surrendered himself hostage to his perfect love.

Scoffing at the notion, Cliff quickly corrected himself.

Perfect? Hardly. There's no such thing as a perfect woman.

When Sunday afternoon bid her farewell, and Sunday evening took hold, Cliff had paced and planned himself into a corner. Unable to force Beth from his mind, Cliff faced his current problem.

Too many people. Too many demands. Somethings got to give. Someone's got to go.

In that one split second, Cliff decided who would go. Picking up the phone, Cliff sealed someone's fate with a one-minute phone call.

"Hi baby, it's me! I need to see you. Can you meet me? Good. Same place as always. Give me two hours, okay? Great, see you there. Love you too, bye."

~~ 25 ~~

When the time was right, Cliff went in search of Susan. He found her dutifully tending to his wife's needs.

"Mom. I feel like pizza for supper. Would you like to join me?"

Before Susan answered, Cliff caught sight of Denny's barely touched dinner tray on the nightstand.

"Make sure Denny eats all her soup, Mom. We don't want her withering away, do we?"

"No, of course not, dear. We are just getting started."

"So how about pizza?"

"That sounds wonderful, Cliff. I'll call and have Georgio's deliver one as soon as I'm finished here. That alright?"

"No need, Mom. I feel like getting out. You just finish up with Denny. I'll wait a little bit, then head on out. Be back with dinner in about an hour. How's that?"

"Sounds perfect."

Moving toward the hall, Cliff watched silently as Susan lifted Denny's tray and put it across her lap. He watched her spoon warm soup into her daughter-in-law's mouth.

Denny felt Cliff's eyes on her as Susan fed her the tainted soup. She didn't want to take any, but she did. She had no choice.

Cliff's watching. He's always watching.

Desperate to block out the world around her, Denny closed her eyes. While that removed Cliff from sight, it did nothing to truly keep him from her.

As Denny drifted toward sleep, the last thing she heard was the sound of her husband.

The sound of him laughing.

Cliff drove past Georgio's Pizza. Heading toward the outskirts of town and the Regional High School, Cliff checked his watch for the third time since he had left home. It didn't really matter that he was a little late because he knew she would be waiting for him, knew she'd wait all night for him. He had been late before, and she always waited. She waited for hours sometimes. *Pathetic!*

Pulling into Town Line Pizza shortly before six, Cliff edged his way through the crowded shop and ordered a pepperoni and green pepper pizza from a petite brunette behind the counter. Looking for a place to sit, but finding none, Cliff told the waitress he would be back in a few minutes to pick up the pizza.

Flashing a full, bright smile, the waitress handed him his change. When their hands touched, Cliff noticed a deep blush had covered her perfectly chiseled cheekbones. He also noticed to fully erect nipples desperate to free themselves from her polyester uniform.

Ooooooo. Not bad! Not bad at all.

Hesitating a moment, Cliff fought to stem the familiar strain he felt growing between his legs.

Not now! Focus! Focus! Focus!

Fully erect, Cliff headed out of the pizza shop without so much as a second glance toward the waitress. The waitress who flagged down her boyfriend the minute Cliff left.

"Steve! Steve, come here, quick!"

A dungaree-clad boy moved from the booth by the window. Approaching the tiny brunette with an eager to please smile, he reached over the counter and gently touched her cheek with his sweaty palm. "What's up, babe?"

"That guy."

"What guy?"

"The guy who just left. Did you see him?"

Turning toward the window, Steve noticed only a set of tail lights pulling away from the curb.

"No, why?"

"That was the cop."

"What cop?"

"From the dance — the parking lot — you know, THE COP."

"Oh, THAT COP."

Standing at the counter, Steve and the girl who had worn the fuzzy pink sweater shared a giggle, just as they had when THAT COP tapped on their car's window the night of the dance.

Cliff killed his lights before pulling into the school's parking lot, then he headed away from where he knew she would be waiting. Pulling his car tight against the brick building, Cliff got out. Pressed tightly against the wall, Cliff listened as music filled the night air. As her fucking country music filled the night air.

Perfect. She won't even hear me coming.

Regretfully for her, she didn't.

Cliff crept along the back of her car, then eased along the passenger side paying special attention to the back door. The very unlocked back door. Finding fate was on his side, Cliff pulled a deep breath, exhaled slowly. When the next song started blaring through the empty parking lot, Cliff pulled the back door open. For a split second, Cliff saw the terrified look in her eyes, still he planted a bullet deep in her head. A head that exploded across her windshield just as the Dixie Chicks belted the chorus to their little tune, *Wide Open Spaces.*

Shutting the door, Cliff quickly retraced his steps. Once safely inside his car and heading out of the parking lot, Cliff realized the irony.

Wide Open Spaces. Bullets make Wide Open Spaces. Yes, they do. They surely do.

Cliff was still laughing when he entered the pizza shop a few minutes later. Stopped laughing when he realized his tiny brunette waitress had left.

Shit! She was cute. Real cute. Had a nice rack too!

~~ 26 ~~

They pulled into the school parking lot, after all it was their place. Their favorite place. Seeing the cop earlier at the pizza shop, gave them ideas. Whenever they had ideas, they headed to their place. Unfortunately, someone else had the same idea. Pulling farther into the parking lot, they found that a car was already parked in their spot. It's lights were off and music blared from its stereo.

Dixie Chicks? Wrong choice of music for making out. Way too loud. Way too country. Way to EVERYTHING!

Disappointed by the circumstances, Steve focused on the parked car. He knew cars. Knew all of his friends' cars anyway, but this car, it didn't belong to any of his friends. It was too nice.

Slowly, quietly, Steve inched his dad's car closer. When he was a couple of car lengths behind the parked car, he realized who it belonged to.

"It's Principal Reedy's."

"Yeah?"

"Yeah. I wonder what she's doing here." Moving forward, Steve flashed his high beams in the direction of his principle's car. Strong, steady beams of light caught the image of a person slumped behind the wheel. Anxiety mounting, Steve honked his horn and waited. The stillness of the night, and the stillness of the body in the parked car turned Steve's anxious feeling into an eerie feeling that danced along his spine.

"Have you got your cell?"

"Yeah, why?"

Honking his horn again, Steve watched, waited, and prayed. Still nothing happened.

Pulling fuzzy pink sweater girl to him, Steve motioned with his head, "Someone's in the car, but they aren't moving."

"What?"

"Watch." He honked again.

When nothing happened, Steve took the cell phone from fuzzy pink sweater girl and punched in 911.

The young lovers held on to each other as rescue personnel pulled their principal from her car. Silently, they watched as she was strapped to a gurney, then loaded into an ambulance. When the pitiful wail of the ambulance echoed off into the distance, they fell to tears.

The teens were still crying when an officer introduced himself, as he led them to a cruiser, as he held the back door open for them. On the way to the station, the cop watched the young couple through his rearview mirror. They held hands the entire trip then during the hour-long questioning as well.

Susan and Cliff enjoyed their pepperoni and green pepper pizza in the den, in front of the television. They were watching an NBA playoff game when a local station broke the news of a shooting at the local high school.

Susan paid special attention.

Cliff tuned most of it out. After all, he already knew the circumstances surrounding the shooting. What he didn't know however, was that the victim was clinging to life.

When her assailant found out, he had only one thought.

Shit!

~~ 27 ~~

When Susan went to bed that evening, Cliff went to work. Taking the gun he used at the high school earlier that evening, Cliff placed it into a brown paper bag before taping it inside the wheel well of Susan's car. Then he popped the hood of his car, and removed the battery cables, rendering it useless.

Useless.

He thought of Denny.

When he thought of Denny, and evil smile crept on to his face.

A motionless Denny lay in the room directly above the driveway. A much-needed sleep called out to her, but noises broke the Stillness of the night. Car noises. Doors, trunks, hoods, being opened, then closed. Muffled footsteps and the occasional jingle of keys seemed to play an accompaniment to the thump, thump, thump of the doors, trunks, and hoods.

Who's out there?

Concentrating on the noises, Denny realized they were coming from the cars parked just below her window.

Someone's in the driveway. In Cliff's car? Susan's? Both?

Wide awake now, Denny waited for more noises. Finally, she heard a very familiar sound. The closing of her back door, followed by footsteps.

Whoever was out there, is in the house now. It's probably Cliff. Maybe Susan.

Within moments, Cliff entered her room. The energy of that once peaceful room took on a very ominous feel. Silently, Denny prepared herself.

*Don't move. Pretend you're asleep. **Don't move!***

Moving close to Denny, Cliff knelt by her bed, gently ran his hand along her cheek as he planted whisper soft kisses along the path he had traced with his fingers. Softly, tenderly, Cliff spoke to his wife.

"Denny. Oh, Denny. Are you in there?"

Denny gave Cliff nothing, but she got so much in return.

Perhaps too much.

"Denny, why didn't you get Page and Preston from school that last day? If you had they would be alive. They should be alive, Denny. They should be with me. It was you who was supposed to go away. Not Page. Not Preston.

111

You, Denny. Only you. That was the plan. But like always, you fucked up. And now, you made me fuck up too.

"I did something tonight, Denny. Something that might jeopardize my entire future, and it's all because of you. Because you just won't go away. God, Denny give it up already will you? There's nothing left for you. Page is gone. Preston is gone. And you killed them. Can't you see there is no reason for you to continue fighting?

"But go ahead, Denny. Fight. And I'll fight too! And I will win. You can't beat me, Denny. Nobody can beat me."

To the outside world Denny appeared lifeless, but on the inside her mind worked over time.

You did something tonight, Cliff? What? Something that might jeopardize your future? And it's my fault? Because I won't go away?

But I will go away Cliff. Just let me out of this prison of drugs. I'll go away. I promise!

Denny tried to forget the rest of what Cliff said. Tried in vain to push his words from her crippled mind. But, just as he said she would, she failed.

You're right, Cliff, there is nothing left for me. Page is gone. Pres is gone. And whatever we had is gone!

Sometimes I feel like giving up, Cliff. But I can't. I don't know why I can't. BUT I CAN'T GIVE UP!

DO YOU HEAR ME, CLIFF? I WON'T GIVE UP. NEVER. NO MATTER HOW MANY TIMES YOU TELL ME IT'S MY FAULT PAGE AND PRES ARE DEAD. I STILL WON'T GIVE UP.

BECAUSE IT'S NOT MY FAULT. I DON'T KNOW HOW I KNOW IT, BUT, I KNOW IT!

Denny was in a deep sleep early the next morning when the slam of the back door startled her awake.

Bright morning sun announced a banner day in the making as it streamed through her bedroom windows. Exhausted and beaten down, Denny welcomed its warmth, beseeched its healing powers. But what she really needed, she knew, was Page and Pres.

Closing her eyes, then she pulled an image of her children's sweet faces forward. Searching for, and finding peace in their loving eyes, Denny opened her shattered heart to it, let it fully embrace her. Let it lift her, carry her. Even though she had vowed the night before to never give up, Denny silently prayed.

Dear Lord, please take me. If I'm worthy of your love, and forgiveness, then save me from this pain.

Please dear Lord, if your plan is to reunite me with my children, then make this the day. Please.

Denny was forced back to the here and now by the sounds of a new day outside her window.

Focusing on the noise, Denny heard car doors opening and closing, then a louder bang from the car. She could hear Cliff cussing and complaining that his car wouldn't start. He told Susan it was just dead.

Rolling into a fetal position, Denny let her one and only thought take up permanent residence in her mind.

Dead — lucky car.

~~ 28 ~~

Susan joined her son on the driveway to see what all the noise was about.

"What's wrong?"

"My car won't start, it's just dead."

"Can you fix it?"

"Don't have enough time right now."

"You want to take mine?"

"I don't want to leave you without wheels, Mom. I'll just take Denny's"

"Don't be silly, Cliff. Take mine. I'm not going anywhere, and besides I don't think you can get Denny's van past yours."

Pretending to survey the situation, Cliff conceded to his mother's point. Of course, he'd already figured all that out, but for his mother's sake, he put on a good show.

"You're right, Mom. Looks like I'll have to take yours. You sure it's okay?"

"Stay right here, Cliff. I'll go get you my keys."

Cliff pulled Susan's car from the driveway, and as expected, he was victorious. He had a plan, executed his plan, and got what he wanted.

What he needed – his mother's car, **and** the gun he had used the night before. Safe and sound, right where he had left it, taped inside wheel well of the car he inched away from his home.

Still, Cliff had work to do. He needed to dispose of the gun, then he needed to return his mother's car.

Simple enough.

That morning, Denny eyed her breakfast tray, found it held a bowl of oatmeal and a cup of tea.

Cliff probably made the tea before he left. Susan must have just made the oatmeal.

Susan held the teacup to Denny, who immediately clamped her mouth shut. Kept it shut tight while lukewarm tea dripped down her chin, onto her chest.

Without so much as a word, Susan put the tea back onto the tray and wiped Denny clean. As she did, she noticed Denny's eyes. She watched intently as they shot welcoming looks toward the bowl of oatmeal.

"Denny, would you like some oatmeal?"

Yes please, just the oatmeal!

Blinking her response, Denny waited for Susan to lift a spoonful of oatmeal and place it against her mouth.

Parting her lips just wide enough for Susan to deposit the warm oatmeal inside her mouth, seemed to send waves of joy through her mother-in-law.

"Oh, Denny. That's wonderful. You're eating again."

Eating? Yes. Drinking? No!

Denny's silent refusal of the tea Susan offered wasn't lost on her mother-in-law. "No tea today? Well that's all right, Denny. Maybe tomorrow."

Maybe not.

Cliff drove past 147 Hummingbird Lane on his way to the station. It didn't matter that Hummingbird Lane wasn't exactly on his way to the station. No, the only thing that mattered was that Cliff wanted to know more about Beth.

Beth. Beth. Beth.

Once past her house, Cliff circled around before pulling to a stop on a hill behind Beth's house that gave him a fairly unobstructed view of the mostly windowed back of her house. Checking his watch, Cliff found that if he didn't leave right away, he would be late for work. But sitting in his mother's car, Cliff knew he had a built-in excuse for being late.

Car trouble. Remember, no rush.

Movement in the main house caught Cliff's attention. Held it, too.

Beth.

Cliff's eyes followed Beth as she moved from room to room on the first floor of her home. Losing sight of her for a moment, he found his hopes dashed, only to have them rebound again when bright light flooded forth from a small upstairs window. Strong beams of light cut through the early dawn, then through him as he realized where Beth was.

The bathroom. Her 118athroomm. Bingo!

Lifting her nightgown over her head, Beth pulled open the shower door and stepped inside. Instantly, Beth was greeted by a soothing warmth. Pressing both palms against the shower walls, Beth stood motionless beneath a gentle spray for several minutes. All the while, she willed tiny knots of tension away.

Sufficiently relaxed, Beth quickly lathered her hair, rinsed, and repeated, before rejuvenating her skin with the tender kiss of Jasmine body scrub. Leaving the warm moist cocoon, Beth stepped from the shower onto a pure white, fluffy bath mat. She quickly wrapped an equally fluffy towel around her hair, before pulling another to dry herself with. Within seconds, the thick fluffy nap of her towel had soaked the last drops of water from her warm, rosy skin.

Moving toward the mirror, Beth swiped it dry with the edge of her towel. Immediately blinded by a flash of light reflecting off the partially steamed glass, Beth followed the light toward the tiny window. Arriving at the window just in time, Beth caught the glimpse of a car on the hillside, as it drove away.

Having pulled a pair of binoculars from the bag he had packed for the outing, Cliff trained them on the object of his desire, just as his sweetness stepped behind a clear glass shower door. Mesmerized, Cliff watched as the silhouetted figure of his newest love leaned toward the steady stream of water, as she lathered, rinsed, touched, and rubbed. He continued watching and wishing he had a view of her body rather than just shoulders and above. However, his imagination allowed him to envision her body. When his beauty finally stepped from the shower, the strain across his pants announced his excitement. He loved the strain, the pull, that his sweet Beth caused.

Lowering the binoculars for a moment, Cliff took a quick look at the rock-hard mound in his pants, before lifting the heavy spy glasses back into place. Training them on the tiny window once again, Cliff was blinded by a ray of sun as it bounced wildly off the lenses, and shot toward the bathroom window.

Shit!

As he pulled from the curb, Cliff replayed the images of his sweet Beth over and over. Much like a film real, fragmented images of Beth through the tiny window as she entered the shower. Her imagined nakedness filled his mind.

Once safely on Pleasant Street, Cliff came to a conclusion; the best part of that morning, was the fact that there was only one car in the circle driveway that morning.

Nothing else.

Even at that early hour when the sun was making its morning appearance, there was only one car.

A midnight blue Volvo.

~~ 29 ~~

Denny refused the soup Susan offered her for lunch, eyed the bowl of green Jello instead.

Susan eagerly complied with Denny's unspoken request before cautioning her that Cliff wouldn't approve if he found out she refused her soup.

"So, it's our little secret, right Denny?"

Secret? Right. Don't worry Susan, I'll never tell. Never!

Denny was thrilled when she heard that Cliff had called to say he would be late getting home from work. It meant she would have another meal without having to worry if Cliff had doctored her food.

But what about tonight? A green pill? White? Purple? What will he give me tonight?

Forcing herself to stay awake that afternoon, Denny hoped she would be fast asleep before Cliff returned home that evening. Thankfully, she was.

Cliff left the station right after he called home. Checking his watch as he pulled off the main road an hour or so later, Cliff relaxed a bit.

Seven-twenty, perfect.

Easing Susan's car down a bumpy dirt road, Cliff pulled it to one side, leaving barely enough room for a car to pass on the other. When Cliff got out of the car, he immediately made his way to the wheel-well and pulled the heavy paper bag free. Relief flooded through him as he felt the gun through the paper and tape. It felt good. Heavy. Dependable.

Tucking the gun into his jacket pocket, Cliff grabbed a flashlight from his bag before heading from the clearing into the heavy woods. Immediately, darkness surrounded him, protected him, calmed him. Breathing in, Cliff pulled the fresh scent of pine deeply into his lungs. Patiently, he let it soothe him, let it remind him how much he loved these woods. How much he loved his father for introducing him to the land he now roamed. Land that spoke to him of its unforgiving nature on every hunting trip he'd ever taken. No more so, than on the last trip they'd taken together.

Pushing the memory of that trip deep within, Cliff focused instead on the lessons his father bestowed upon him in these woods. Lessons like respect — for the woods and its inhabitants, especially those whose lives they held in the palms of their hands.

With each carefully placed step, Cliff thought of the many other lessons his father shared with him in those woods. Lessons like how to choose, stalk, then kill your prey without so much as a hint of what was on your mind.

So many times he had failed at those lessons, especially the ones on stalking prey. But on the day he'd found success, the day of his first kill, well, that day he felt like a man. Like a hunter. A hunter who's prey never saw what was coming.

Yes, he was the hunter then, but unfortunately, he felt more like the hunted now. The weight of the gun tapping against his side made him feel that way. After all, the gun was a reminder, a constant reminder of why he felt hunted. He had made mistakes. Two huge mistakes. His wife, and his lover.

Focusing on the two women who had offered him their lives, their pathetic, cheap lives, only infuriated Cliff. He hated them. Their weakness, their uselessness. They were nothing, their lives meant nothing. It was up to him to let them, and the world, know what their lives meant. That's why he took what he wanted from them, and when he'd tired of them, he'd tried to end their cheap, pathetic lives. Unfortunately, ending those lives proved more difficult than he'd hoped. And those difficulties caused him to fail, to make mistakes. Two huge mistakes. Mistakes who refused to die, refused to set him free.

But soon he would be free. Free from the hatred he felt for them. Free from the hatred he felt for himself. Once they were gone, he'd be free. Free to take the only thing left for him to take.

Beth!

Cliff tossed the brown paper bag into Lake Chumgawanga, listened as it bubbled to the silty bottom. With that one act, Cliff knew he'd begun correcting his mistakes. With that one act, Cliff became victorious.

Using the flashlight to pierce the dark that enveloped him, Cliff quickly retraced his steps. Once back on the highway, Cliff tuned out his troubles as his thoughts turned to his new love.

Beth.

When Cliff slid back into town around nine that evening, he decided it was too late to wash the mud and debris from Susan's car, but not too late to swing past Beth's house.

No, it wasn't too late for that, nor would it ever be.

Cliff didn't pull to the curb outside Beth's house, he didn't need to. He saw what he saw, and liked what he saw.

The main house was dark, through and through. No one was home. Still, he could see his sweet, sweet Beth. Sitting at an antique desk in the small brick building, Beth was completely unaware that her true love sent loving looks her way. All alone in her little brick building, she waited for him. Only him.

Soon my love. Very, very soon.

124

Beth caught the reflection of headlights moving slowly past her house. Her heart leapt with the hope it might be Philip, then it sank when she realized the light had come from the street, not the driveway. Hindered by the darkness, Beth tried in vain to make out what type of car it was that moved so slowly past her house.

Is it Philip?

Straining for a closer look, Beth settled for the last gleam of tail lights before realizing they weren't from Philip's BMW. Her BMW.

What did it matter? His car, her car. His life, her life. They weren't together anymore. That was all that mattered.

That, and for the first time since Philip left, she felt something.

Alone.

She felt terribly alone .

~~ 30 ~~

When Cliff woke the next day, he woke to a day of questions. They started at breakfast.

"Cliff, is there any news on the shooting?"

"News?"

"You know, is there a suspect or anything like that?"

"I don't know, Mom. I don't work violent crimes."

"I know, Cliff. But, being at the station I thought maybe you heard something."

"Sorry."

With that, Cliff quickly changed the subject.

"Mom, I got in pretty late last night, so I haven't worked on my car yet. Any chance I could use yours again today?"

"Sure. But, could you do me a favor?"

"What favor?"

"Could you wash it before you bring it back tonight? It's filthy."

"It is?"

"Sure looked it when I went out to get the paper this morning."

Sticking his nose further into the paper, Cliff silently admonished himself for the oversight.

Stupid. Stupid. A mistake like that could prove costly.

Pulled from his thoughts, Cliff tuned into his mother's rambling.

"Did you hear me, Cliff? Denny had a wonderful day, yesterday."

His curiosity peeked, Cliff folded the paper and looked to his mother's chipper face.

"Really? How so?"

"She was more alert than I've seen her in weeks. I think she even communicated with me."

"She spoke?"

"No, no. But, there are other ways of communicating, without using words, you know."

"No, I didn't know."

"Well, there are. Take yesterday, for example, Denny used her eyes to tell me what she wanted."

"Oatmeal and jello."

"So she ate?"

"Yes."

"And her soup. Did she eat her soup, too?"

Susan lied. "Oh yes, every drop."

"Good. That's very good, Mom."

Denny lay awake hoping she'd hear the comforting slam of the back door that announced Cliff's departure. Unfortunately, she heard something else.

"Good morning, Denny."

Denny stiffened at the sound of his voice, then she remained still. Perfectly still.

"I know you're awake Denny, so don't try to fool me."

Moving around the bed, Cliff sat close to his wife. "Denny. Oh, Denny, open your eyes."

Denny clamped her eyes even tighter.

"Open your eyes dammit, or I'll open them for you."

At her husband's mercy, Denny silently willed her mother-in-law upstairs.

*Susan! Please, Susan, come upstairs. I **need** you!*

Still praying for Susan, Denny was startled by the harsh tone of Cliff's next words.

"Open your eyes. Now!"

When Denny obeyed, she found Cliff sitting very near her, holding a glass of water.

Oh, no! Pills.

"It's time for your medication, Denny. Mom says you were more alert yesterday, so your medication must be working. I'm so pleased, Denny. You must be pleased, too."

Instinctively, Denny inched away from Cliff.

"Look at that, you're moving. That's wonderful."

Without missing a beat, Cliff raised his voice again. **"Sit up and take your pills!"**

"Cliff! What on earth are you doing?"

"I'm trying to give Denny her medicine. Why?"

"You yelled at her."

"I did? I yelled at Denny? I didn't mean to, I don't even remember yelling."

Joining her son on the other side of the room, Susan made a move to touch him. Immediately, Cliff pulled away and walked around the bed to get closer to Denny, all the while addressing his frail wife.

"Denny, Mom said you're making progress. Let's keep it going."

Lifting Denny's head and shoulders off the mattress, Cliff motioned, then asked his mother for help. "Mom, get the other side, will you?"

Working together, they pulled Denny into a sitting position, while Cliff continued his cajoling.

"Come on Denny, take your medicine."

Joining her son, Susan encouraged her daughter-in-law, as she helped Cliff slide the pills into Denny's mouth.

"That's a girl, now swallow."

Turning helpless, tormented eyes toward Susan, Denny prayed that she would see the words that tumbled freely inside her head.

Please, Susan. Help me! Please.

As expected, Denny's silent plea went unnoticed.

Cliff faced a second round of questions shortly after he arrived at the station that morning. He hadn't even made it to the locker room when Sgt. Michael Carbone of the violent crimes division stopped him.

"Hey Cliff, how's it going?"

"It's going."

"Good. You got a minute?"

"Sure. What's up?"

"I'm working the high school shooting, and I'm hoping you can help me."

"If there's a drug connection, I'm your man."

"Drugs? Naw."

Sgt. Carbone pulled a notebook from his shirt pocket, flipped through several pages, found what he wanted to discuss.

"You knew the victim."

"Knew?"

"Knew, worked for, whatever."

"Sure, I guess I knew her. I worked for her, anyway."

"Extra pay jobs?"

"Yeah, dances, athletic events, that sort of thing."

"What was she like?"

"Easy to work for. She said what she wanted, then stayed out of the way while you made sure she got it."

"When was the last time you worked for her?"

"Couple weeks ago."

"So, that was the last time you saw her?"

"Yeah. Hey, what's this all about, Mike?"

"Nothing. Just collecting background, you know."

Yeah, I know, and what I know is you ain't got shit, Mike, and you never will.

Cliff kept a low profile the rest of that week, at home, and at the station.

That thrilled Denny to no end, but when Cliff didn't bring her morning or evening pills, and she still felt the same, Denny faced the cold, hard truth. Cliff was putting them in her food. Food that Susan dutifully delivered three times a day. Food that made her sleepy, or confused, or gave her horrible dreams.

That Thursday, Susan greeted Beth on the driveway.

"Good morning, Susan. How's Denny?"

"About the same."

"Really? No improvement?"

"Well, there was some improvement earlier this week, but she seems to have slipped again."

"Slipped? Hmm."

The 'slipped' terminology conjured up a vision of Denny on a roller-coaster, slowly pulling herself up, only to have the car slip away from her on a downward slope. Within a few minutes, Beth's vision brought forth a question.

"Susan, have you noticed anything about Denny that would give insight into why she gets better? Or why she declines?"

Susan's silence raised Beth's hackles just a bit. "Susan, if there's something, anything, please tell me."

"Well, Denny had a wonderful day Monday."

"And Tuesday?"

"Not so good. Cliff had some trouble giving Denny her medication Tuesday morning. And ..."

"And, what?"

"Well, he lost his temper with her."

"What? How so?"

"He yelled at Denny."

"You heard him?"

"Yes. I was just walking into the room and he yelled 'sit up and take your pills', or something like that."

"What did you say?"

"I don't remember exactly, but I let Cliff know in no uncertain terms that he was out of line, and that he'd better not do it again."

"And, how did he respond to that?"

"He apologized."

"But?"

"Dr. Malone, the thing that concerns me is that Cliff said he hadn't realized he'd raised his voice at Denny. Unfortunately, I believe him."

"Why?"

"Well for one thing, I've never heard Cliff raise his voice to Denny before, and when I admonished him for his behavior, he seemed so out of it. Like he really didn't know he'd raised his voice."

"How was he after the incident?"

"He seemed fine. He was attentive, helpful, and supportive."

"And since then?"

"I haven't really seen much of him, but when I do, he seems fine."

"Why haven't you seen much of him?"

"He's spent a lot of time in his study this week. I think he's preoccupied with work."

"That could explain the outburst."

"Yes, I suppose you're right. Of course, you're right. Cliff's been under a great deal of pressure with Denny, and I'm sure the shooting at the high school has him under stress as well."

"Shooting? Oh, that's right, your son is a police officer, right?"

"Yes."

"And, he's working on the shooting case?"

"Well, not directly, but I'm sure the whole department is involved in the investigation. How could they not be? It's so tragic."

"Yes, tragic. Very tragic."

When Cliff felt the time was right, he pulled his unmarked car onto the circular driveway. Having found Beth at his home twice before on Thursdays, he was pretty confident she would be there again that day. Since he was a betting man, he rolled the dice.

Looks like I'm a winner!

Leaving the engine running, Cliff checked his watch, then made tracks toward the main house. Taking a quick peek into the back door, Cliff moved on to the wrap around porch for a full view of Beth's home. What he found was a magnificent view of the entire first floor of the stately abode. The layout was simple, direct, and grand.

Standing opposite the back door once again, Cliff could see into a tiny mudroom that led to a huge chef's kitchen. Off the kitchen was a vaulted-ceiling dining room, flanked on one side by a turn of the century coal stove. Opposite the dining room was an antique filled living room, separated by a small foyer and grand mahogany staircase that led to the upstairs.

Moving along the porch toward the final set of windows, Cliff found they offered a view of what he assumed was a three-season porch, crammed tight with overstuffed, fluffy, soft furniture upholstered in a deep red, coral, and pumpkin floral pattern.

Retracing his steps so he faced the living room, Cliff took in the sight of a room that commanded attention. Sturdy and expensive antiques were placed around a floor to ceiling fireplace in a comfortable seating arrangement. None of the furniture seemed comfortable or inviting despite the well-used look of the fireplace.

What a shame.

Staring at the fireplace, Cliff decided it was the focal point of the room, if not the entire house. Complete with a hand carved mahogany mantle that stretched proudly from east to west, the fireplace matched a center staircase banister and crown molding that encircled the room perfectly.

Expensive. Really expensive.

Checking his watch again, Cliff hopped off the porch and made his way along a brick inlaid walkway toward the small brick building. Taking his place outside the wall-to-wall windows, Cliff found he had a perfect view into Beth's mystery world. A world guarded by a state-of-the-art security system. Cupping his hands along the sides of his face, Cliff leaned against the glass and quickly assessed the security panel. A thrilling shot of adrenaline pulsed through him when he found it matched the one he had seen on the mud room wall inside the main house. Same size, same red light.

Too bad it's activated.

Pressing his face even tighter against the window, Cliff saw that the layout of the small brick building was simple. It contained an office area, sitting room, and at the far end, there was another door.

Another room? I wonder what my sweet Beth does in that other room? Let's go find out.

Running out of time, Cliff moved to the back of the building. Shrubs, bushes, plants of all kinds, hugged the sturdy brick walls, making it difficult for him to walk. Determined, he pressed on, pushed his way through the tough, sturdy plants. Eventually, his efforts paid off when he found a window cut into the thick brick façade. A window he figured would offer a clear view into the back room if he could access it. Unfortunately, the window was just beyond Cliff's reach.

Using the one and only thing at his disposal, Cliff placed his weight on the sturdiest part of a laurel bush and raised himself within reach of the window. Grabbing hold of the window ledge, Beth's stalker peered into the back room.

For all his efforts, Cliff was a bit disappointed to find that the small room was nothing more than another sitting area. An area where soft, sage green walls stood guard over rich upholstered chairs, a small sofa, and an overstuffed couch. Plants, books, statues, and tiny framed writings filled every inch of floor and table tops. Pictures hung from every wall, and unlike any other room he had seen that day, he found this room had a very homey, comfortable feel to it.

It's a haven. A cozy little haven. My Beth's haven.

Hopping from the bush, Cliff continued his walk around the brick building. On the far side, he found a window similar to the one in back, but this window offered a better view and easier access to Beth's mystery world. Moving a few steps up and embankment, Cliff peaked into the tiny window and to his pleasure, he found that he was looking at the side view of the front office area.

Breaking into an ear-to-ear grin, Cliff decided he liked this view of Beth's office area the best. After all, it fit his plans.

See you soon, baby.

~~ 32 ~~

When Beth entered Denny's room shortly after 9:00 that morning, she watched as Denny flinched then pulled tightly into a fetal position. Moving from her usual spot, Beth stood with the bright Sun against her back before addressing Denny.

"Denny, it's me, Beth."

A slight relaxation was obvious, but still Denny kept her eyes closed tightly.

"Denny. Can you open your eyes?"

Nothing.

"Please, Denny, I'd like to check your eyes, see if you're all right."

Denny opened her eyes, quickly closed them when Beth bent to examine her and bright Sun streamed through the window. Standing to block the sun, Beth busied herself with the window shade. When it was fully closed, she continued.

"There, that should do it. You can open your eyes now Denny."

When Denny opened them, giant tears slid down her cheeks.

"Denny, are you sad?"

Nothing.

"About Page and Preston?"

Angry moans left Denny's body, their intensity startled Beth. Clearly on the wrong track, Beth regrouped, and began again.

"Okay, Denny. I understand. This isn't about Page and Preston."

Another guttural moan.

"And ... you aren't sad?"

Another moan, this time softer, pleading.

"Okay. Umm. Denny when I came in a few minutes ago, you stiffened. Are you scared?"

Frantic blinking sent a River of Tears along Denny's cheeks.

"You're scared?"

Remembering Susan's earlier words, Beth took a stab.

"Are you afraid of Cliff?"

Wide, terrified eyes and a tormented groan left no room for doubt in Beth's mind.

"Because Cliff yelled at you?"

A nod.

Moving onto Denny's bed, Beth took hold of her clenched hand, and began massaging her tightly cramped fingers.

"Susan told me, Denny, about Cliff's outburst the other morning. Did he scare you, Denny?"

Yes, he scares me. Especially when I won't take the pills. But it's really the pills that scare me.

THERE'S SOMETHING WRONG WITH THE PILLS. HELP ME! PLEASE!

Beth watched as Denny's eyes shot back and forth like balls in a pinball machine. Every so often, Denny's eyes would stop, only to begin the rapid movement once again. It was clear to Beth that Denny was in search of something, clear that she had found it when she turned wide, pleading eyes toward Beth.

"You need something from me?"

Blinking once again, Denny let silent tears fill in the blanks of how badly she was in need of Beth's help.

For more than an hour, Beth massaged Denny's legs, arms, shoulders, hands, and feet. All the while she carried on a one-sided conversation with Denny. Focusing on Denny's physical responses, it wasn't long before she knew that Cliff was the trigger that sent Denny spiraling downward. Not even the mention of Page or Preston or their last day seemed to unnerve Denny as much as the mere mention of Cliff's name did.

Too dangerous to push on, Beth omitted Cliff's name from the remainder of their session. That seemed to help Denny in the short run, but Beth knew there was a reservoir of fear in Denny. She also knew that it would eventually break free.

After instructing Susan to assist Cliff with Denny whenever possible, Beth headed home.

Surprised to find a car parked on the circle driveway, Beth found she was even more surprised by her reaction to it. Her heart racing, Beth exited the Volvo and joined her soon to be ex-husband on the wrap-around porch.

"Philip. I wasn't expecting you."

God, Philip. It's great to see you.

"I should have called."

"No, no. It's alright."

You look wonderful.

"Beth, do you have a few minutes? We need to talk."

"Sure. Come on in."

He wants to talk. Maybe he's changed his mind. Please, please let it be that he's changed his mind .

~~ 33 ~~

That night when Beth retired, she retired with hopeful thoughts. Her conversation with Philip was light, friendly, and he admitted freely that he missed her.

She gathered that from the way he talked, moved, and stared. But it was far more important that he told her that he missed her. REALLY MISSED HER.

Just as it was important for her to tell him, and she told him because she misses him too REALLY MISSES HIM. More than she ever imagined possible.

Maybe that's the point of this separation. Maybe it won't lead to divorce. Maybe Philip's right. Maybe all we needed was some time and space to think about what's really important. To decide what we're willing to sacrifice so we can be together. Always.

His words had 'ung hollow when he first said them the night he left. But now as she lay alone in their bed, without him, she wasn't so sure. Thinking about the sacrifices they would each have to make in order to stay together once seemed so overwhelming. But now, well now she realized that the sacrifices came down to one thing. Time. Taking time from their prospective jobs. Giving time to each other.

Pulling Philip's pillow to her, Beth lay her face in its soft embrace, and let their time apart take its toll.

Cliff tested Susan at dinner that night.

"How was your day, Mom?"

"Like any other, dear."

"Really? No visitors today?"

"Visitors?"

"Beth. Doesn't Beth usually come by on Thursdays?"

"Does she? Thursdays?"

"Well, the two times I saw her were Thursdays. Maybe she comes other days, too?"

"NO!" Susan snapped.

Taken aback by the sudden outburst, Cliff eased a bit.

"God, Mom, what's with you?"

Surprisingly, silence was his mother's only response.

"Mom, are you alright? I mean, you seem sort of jumpy."

"I'm fine. I guess I've just been cooped up too long."

"Well, I can fix that."

Although it only took him seconds to reconnect the battery cables he'd loosened earlier that week, Cliff played it safe by staying out on the driveway for almost an hour.

Make it look good, Cliffy. Don't want Mommy to think you pulled a fast one!

As instructed by Beth, Susan followed Cliff to Denny's room that night, and again the next morning. Paying special attention to Denny as Cliff medicated her, Susan could easily see that Denny did not want her medication.

"Cliff, it looks like Denny doesn't want her pills."

"So?"

"Well maybe she's trying to tell us something."

"Like?"

"Maybe she doesn't need them anymore. Maybe we should call Dr. Valez, have him check in on Denny."

"No."

"Why not?"

"Mom, there's no change in Denny. Why make Dr. Valez come all this way to tell us what we already know?"

"But," Susan was quickly interrupted by her son.

"No buts, Mom. At least not now. How about we give it another couple of weeks, if there's no change by then, I'll call. Okay?"

"Okay, Cliff."

Listening to the conversation, Denny's heart beat wildly in her chest. When Susan suggested that Dr. Valez come back to see her, she felt hopeful. But when Cliff refused the suggestion, her hopes were soon dashed.

~~ 34 ~~

Cliff snuck into Denny's room several times over the next few days, unaccompanied by Susan. Each time, he brought the tiny green pills with him.

Weary from her never-ending battle, Denny dutifully took the pills that Cliff placed onto her tongue. Then, with her husband by her side, Denny would wait for sleep to take her prisoner, for dreams to find and shackle her, for death to greet her. She knew it was only a matter of time.

Cliff knew it too.

Cliff left his home early Wednesday morning. Very early. With Darkness still shrouding the upscale neighborhood, he slowly moved past 147 Hummingbird Lane. Pleased when he found it as dark inside as it was outside, Cliff put his plan into motion.

Still sleeping, honey? Perfect.

Cliff parked his car out of sight from Beth's house and made his way quietly through still dark back yards. Hopping a fence or two and slipping along perfectly manicured lawns, he had a thought.

The neighborhood was quiet. Very quiet. Hmm. No dogs. Probably hundreds of security systems, but no dogs. Anyone in law enforcement will tell you there's no better protection than a dog.

As he moved unchallenged, Cliff proved that point.

He proved his point again when he tackled his final obstacle. Pushing his way through the thick laurel and holly bushes that bordered Beth's property from that of her neighbors, Cliff found that they too, were unable to keep him from his love. His prey. Once free from the woody embrace of laurel and holly, Cliff found himself on the back side of the small brick building. Found himself just where he wanted to be. Quietly Cliff moved along the brick structure to the far end. Rounding the corner, he continued moving until he was just outside the small window he found the last time he surveyed Beth's property. Peeking through the window, Cliff couldn't help but smile when he realized how perfect his plan was. He was still smiling when Beth emerged from her house almost an hour later.

Moving toward the small brick building, coffee cup in one hand, newspaper in the other, Beth juggled her load before slipping a shiny gold key into the lock. Pushing the door open, Beth

147

dropped her load onto a tall file cabinet before giving her stalker what he'd come for.

Cliff watched with bated breath as Beth made her way toward the small brick building — as she opened her office door — as she punched her security code into the panel — as the light turned from red to Green.

And just like that, Cliff had what he had come for.

Beth's security code.

8563.

Burning those four little numbers into his brain, Cliff retraced his steps along the back of the small brick building and through Beth's neighbor's yard. If anyone had heard Cliff as he made his way to his car, they would have heard him recite a little poem for his love, a poem that went something like this: *8563. 8563. Pretty soon Beth, I'll come to thee.*

~~ 35 ~~

Denny wracked her brain trying to remember the events of the past few days. For all her efforts, she came up with only one thing. Pills.

There were morning pills, evening pills, and in between those, there were more pills. Since her children's deaths, it seemed that her whole existence centered around pills. Pills, pills, and more pills.

Pills that removed Denny from the world around her, kept her prisoner. Until that following Thursday, that is.

When Beth found Denny in her usual fetal position that morning, she immediately began tending to Denny's stiff muscles. Tenderly, yet purposefully, Beth rubbed life into Denny's feet, legs, shoulders, arms, and hands.

Hands that were clenched tightly around countless little pills that tumbled free as Beth loosened Denny's death like grip.

Astounded at the colorful display of pills that fell onto Denny's wrinkled, limp bed sheet, Beth gingerly fingered a lot. There were white oval pills, shiny purple pills, and tiny green pills. Moving them from side to side, Beth identified the white oval pills.

Over the counter pain pills.

Shiny purple pills.

Sedative.

The green ones however, puzzled her. Lifting one to survey it more closely, Beth readily admitted that she had absolutely no clue what the tiny green pills were. But she decided she better find out.

Beth left Denny, and went in search of Susan. As expected, she found her in the kitchen reading the morning paper.

"Finished already?"

"No."

Beth's tone wasn't lost on Susan. "Dr. Malone, is something wrong?"

"I'm not sure."

"Oh?"

"Susan, I'd like to see Denny's prescriptions."

"But, you've already seen them."

"I'd still like to see them again, please."

Checking every cupboard and drawer, Susan eventually made the announcement Beth expected.

"They're not here. I don't understand where they could be."

"Susan, who gives Denny her medication?"

"Cliff does."

"Could he have moved them? Maybe run out?"

"I honestly don't know."

Impossible to hide her disappointment or concern, Beth simply stared at Denny's mother-in-law.

"Dr. Malone, is something wrong? Why do you need to see Denny's medication?"

"I think you should come with me, Mrs. Jameson."

Entering Denny's room, they took space on either side of the seemingly lifeless form on the bed.

"Dr. Malone, maybe we should leave. She's sleeping."

"No, she's pretending."

"What?"

Ignoring Susan, Beth spoke directly to Denny.

"Denny, open your eyes."

It took a moment, but Denny's eyes finally popped open.

Burning hot anger simmered with a sense of betrayal and confusion. When Susan spoke, she found it impossible to mask her feelings. "She's been faking? All this time? Just look what she has put us all through! How …"

Beth interrupted Susan's rant by saying "No, absolutely not faking. But there has been some playing possum though."

"What? Why?"

Opening her hand, Beth showed a dozen or more pills to Susan.

"What are those?"

"Denny's medication."

"She hasn't been taking it?"

"It looks that way."

"For how long?"

Shrugging her shoulders, Beth turned and addressed Denny. "How long, Denny?"

Nothing.

Panic shot through Susan as the full extent of what she was learning hit her.

"Cliff's going to be upset when he finds out Denny hasn't been taking her pills. Very upset!"

"Susan, there has to be a reason why Denny didn't take her pills, I'd like to find out what that reason is."

"How?"

"I need to see her prescriptions."

"I don't understand. You saw me look for them, I don't know where they are. How will seeing the prescriptions help you know?"

"Well, there are three different types of pills here. I can identify two of them, but the third … I haven't got a clue what it might be."

"Three? But, Dr. Valez only prescribed two."

Beth held up a white oval pill.

"This is an over-the-counter pain medication."

"Then the other two should be the ones Dr. Valez prescribed."

Unable to suppress her emotions, Denny let out an animal-like growl.

Jumping away from the bed, Susan stared frightfully at her daughter-in-law.

"What's she doing? Is that because she stopped her medicine?"

As if to answer for herself, Denny released another deafening growl.

Ignoring Susan, Beth turned her attention to Denny. Fixed on her eye movements, her body thrashing, her moans and groans. Using herself in as many ways as possible, Denny let them know she was ready to communicate.

"Susan, Denny's obviously trying to tell us something."

Stunned by the creature laying before her, Susan fully realized for the first time, that words really weren't needed if someone wanted to communicate.

~~ 36 ~~

Outside Denny's room, the women filled the empty hallway with their presence and their confusion.

"Susan, I **really** need to see Denny's prescriptions."

"I don't have them, and I don't know where Cliff keeps them."

"Can we check his room, maybe his study?"

"WHAT? I don't want to invade my son's privacy like that."

"Susan, I think there's a problem with the medication Cliff's been giving Denny."

"A problem? What kind of problem?"

"Maybe there was a mix-up at the pharmacy, or with the prescriptions, but some of the pills Denny's been getting look funny to me."

"A mix-up? Oh dear. Well, in that case, I suppose we can take a quick peek in Cliff's room."

Following Susan down the narrow hall, Beth hoped beyond hope that they would find there had been a pharmacy mistake. Hoped, but somehow, she didn't believe that would be the case.

Denny's pills were tucked deep in Cliff's top dresser drawer. Unscrewing the bottle with the earliest prescription day, Beth expected to find the sedative Dr. Valez prescribed. Inside however, Beth found white oval shaped pills.

Over the counter pain reliever?

Compelled to continue, Beth unscrewed the second bottle, the one who's label said she would find antidepressants inside. Inside this bottle, Beth found a generous supply of shiny purple pills.

Sedatives.

Pouring some of the oval pills from the first bottle into her hand, Beth addressed Susan. "See these?"

"Yes."

"These are over-the-counter pain relievers."

Pouring the shiny purple pills from the second bottle into her hand, Beth continued, "And these?"

"Yes."

"These are sedatives. The sedatives prescribed by Dr. Valez."

Holding up the first bottle, Beth pointed to the prescription. "They belong in this bottle - **not this bottle.**"

Working the information over and over in her mind, Susan came up with a perfectly plausible explanation for the mix-up.

"Cliff must have spilled them, then put them back into the wrong bottles, that's all."

Reaching into her pocket, Beth pulled several tiny green pills free. "Okay, then, how do we explain these?"

"Well, they must be the antidepressants Dr. Valez prescribed."

"No, I'm afraid they're not."

"Then what are they?"

"I haven't the faintest idea. Nor do I have any idea where the antidepressants Dr. Valez prescribed are."

Beth stormed down the hall toward Denny's room. It took a few seconds, but Susan eventually followed her.

"Dr. Malone, wait, please. I'm sure there's a reasonable explanation."

"Susan, I need your help."

"Please, Dr. Malone, let's wait before we jump to any conclusions. I'm sure Cliff has a perfectly logical explanation for the mix-up."

"Really? Because the only explanation I can come up with is that someone has tampered with Denny's medication."

Beth's proclamation sent Denny wild.

"Dr. Malone, please! You're upsetting Denny. Please stop!"

Instead of calming her daughter-in-law, Susan's words enraged an already frantic Denny. Thrashing wildly on her rumpled bed, Denny shot menacing looks and hateful hisses toward her mother-in-law.

Moving close to Denny, Beth softly, soothingly addressed her client.

"Denny. Do you think there's a problem with your medication?"

Wild thrashing and rapidly blinking eyes were Denny's response.

"Do you think someone's giving you the wrong medication?"

Thrashing, blinking, thrashing, and more blinking.

"Do you think someone's doing this to cause you harm?"

Thrashing, blinking, groaning, hissing.

"Do you know who that someone is?"

Thrashing, blinking, groaning, moaning.

"Is it your husband, Cliff?"

With those five simple words, Denny freed herself from her prison of drugs.

"YES!"

In a state of shock, Susan barely heard, barely registered anything but Denny's scream. Still, Beth tried to reach her, needed to reach her.

"Susan! Susan!"

As the fog lifted from Susan's mind, she found Beth desperately trying to lift Denny to a sitting position.

"What are you doing?"

"Getting her out of here."

"WHAT?"

"I'm taking Denny out of this house."

"You can't, I won't allow you to."

Pulling a cell phone from her pocket, Beth punched in two numbers, then held her finger above the final 1 in 911.

"Dr. Malone, please. Don't call the police."

"I don't want to, but I will. Mrs. Jameson, I hope there is a logical explanation for this mix-up. Really, I do, but I'm not willing to risk Denny by leaving her here until we find out. So, either help me get her out of here, or try to stop me from calling the police. Those are your only two options."

"But what will I tell Cliff?"

"The truth! If this is all a huge mistake, then he will want to find out what's happened here just as much as we do. Besides, how could he possibly object to our acting in the best interest of his wife?"

Cliff checked his watch as he drove past 147 Hummingbird Lane. Ten thirty-five. Having seen Beth at his house as late as eleven, he hoped she would be there until at least then, that Thursday morning. If so, he should have enough time for his plan. Still, he knew he was cutting it close. Really close.

Parking his car out of the way, Cliff back-tracked on foot through neighboring yards before making his way behind the small brick building. Pushing through thick heavy foliage, Cliff made his way to the front door, quickly popped the lock, then headed for the security panel.

Confidently, he punched in the magic numbers.

8563.

Just as he'd expected, the red light turned green.

Bingo!

Without hesitation, Cliff headed to Beth's antique desk. Pulling the heavy roll-top up, he was immediately greeted by a blotter-style calendar. Scanning the hand-written entries, Cliff noticed Denny's name and the numbers 9-11 written on every Thursday. Realizing for the first time that Beth had been to see Denny many more times than the two he was aware of, as well as the fact that Beth didn't just 'stop in' to see how Denny was doing, sent his adrenaline pumping.

Calm down. Focus. Focus.

Nervously, Cliff checked his watch again.

Ten-forty.

Setting the alarm on his watch for fifteen minutes, Cliff resumed his search. Having lost interest in the calendar, Cliff pulled open the top drawer of Beth's desk. Sitting center-stage was an assortment of pens, pencils, clips, loose change, and a generous supply of business cards. Pulling one from the pile, Cliff learned what his sweet, sweet Beth did for a living. The simple card announced it loud and clear.

Beth A. Malone, Psychologist

The bitch is a therapist.

Scripted words beneath Beth's name clarified her role even further.

Specialist in Post Traumatic Stress Disorders through Interpretive Communication.

As though struck by a bolt of lightning, Cliff thought back to a comment his mother made earlier that week.

"I think Denny communicated with me. No, she didn't speak, but there are other ways of communicating you know. Take yesterday, Denny used her eyes to tell me what she wanted."

Angrily, Cliff stuffed Beth's business card into his pocket and began pulling at the other desk drawers.

Locked. Shit!

Pushing away from the desk, Cliff moved to the far side of the office space, and pulled at several file drawers before realizing they too, were locked. Checking his watch one more time, Cliff found he had just over 7 minutes left before his alarm went off.

Shit. Not enough time.

Slamming his hand across the sturdy steel, Cliff announced to the world what he thought of Denny, Beth, and his mother.

Fucking bitches!

His anger driving him on, Cliff moved through the sitting area toward the back room. The smell of sweet incense greeted him, teased him, insulted him. Standing in the doorway, Cliff finally realized the obvious. Unable to believe he had missed the obvious signs when he peeked in the back window at this room, Cliff refused to miss the signs this time. Standing smack dab in the middle of Beth's cozy little haven was the proverbial shrink couch.

Storming to the security panel, Cliff punched in Beth's code, before bolting out the front door. Lost in his anger, Cliff headed across the driveway, only to remember he had parked his car on some God forsaken side street.

Beth sped away from Denny's just before 11:00. Checking her rear-view mirror, she caught Denny's reflection out of the corner of her eye. Barely occupying a third of the backseat, Denny watched childlike as the world moved past her.

Just knowing that Denny was safe did wonders for Beth's troubled heart. It not only freed her from guilt and fear, but it reinforced that she had done the right thing. The only thing. Still, she couldn't ease the sense of doom that lapped at her like a thirsty dog.

Pulling her cell phone from her pocket, Beth steadied herself before punching a series of numbers into the tiny contraption.

The mere sound of his voice caused Beth to lose her composure.

"Philip Malone."

"Philip, I need you."

"What? When?"

"Now."

"Right now? Where?"

"Meet me at the house, I'll be there in fifteen minutes."

When Beth hung up, she cried a little. Seeing Beth upset made Denny cry a little, too.

If Philip had known what Beth had done, he might have cried a little, too. Instead, he rushed to be with his wife.

Philip was waiting for her when she pulled her midnight blue Volvo onto the driveway. Racing to her car, he ripped open the driver's side door and started with the questions that had worried him since the tearful phone call.

"Beth, what is it? What's the matter?"

It was Denny who responded to his question, with an animal like growl.

Bending close to Beth, Philip looked into the back seat at the frightened figure.

"Beth who is she? What's wrong with her?"

"She's a client."

"What?"

"Philip. Help me get her inside, will you?"

Working together, they pulled Denny from the car. With no effort at all, Philip lifted Denny into his arms, and headed toward the small brick building.

"Philip wait, bring her into the house."

"What? You're bringing her inside ... inside the house?"

"She's going to be staying with me for a while."

"What?"

Beth could only imagine what was going through Philip's mind as he carried Denny up the back steps. She wondered if he thought about Denny at all. More likely, Philip thought about Beth, and her inability to separate from her work. It was the main problem between them. Philip's problem anyway.

~~ 38 ~~

Philip waited outside the guest room while Beth tended to Denny. Pulling a swimsuit on to Denny, Beth couldn't help but notice that her skin and bones barely kept the fabric in place. Couldn't help but notice Philip's reaction to Denny's gaunt body as he helped her get Denny into the shower and onto a sturdy plastic bench. Having used the bench when she cared for her mother after her first stroke, Beth was adept at caring for an invalid. Just seeing Denny sitting on the bench, was enough to release a flood of memories.

After caring for Denny in the most gentle and dignified manner, Beth escorted a minimally functioning Denny to the guest room. It was there that Beth found Philip, waiting by a window. Soft afternoon light haloed him, and under the circumstances, Beth thought it seemed highly appropriate.

Within minutes of resting her head on the pillow, Denny was fast asleep, and Beth and Philip were in the kitchen sitting on opposite sides of an oak island.

Philip was waiting for an explanation, but when none seemed imminent, he began their conversation with one well-placed word.

"Well?"

"Denny's a client. She suffered a terrible loss recently. Her children were killed in that bus accident a couple of months ago."

"Children? She lost more than one child?"

"Yes, a son and a daughter."

"Oh my God!"

After an appropriate moment of silence, Beth continued.

"Anyway, I've been seeing Denny at her home on Thursdays. We were making progress. She had even begun speaking at one point, then all of a sudden, bam! Nothing."

"Nothing?"

"No nothing. All forms of communication stopped. She became practically catatonic."

"Why?"

"Ah, now that's an interesting question. At first, I thought maybe we went too fast with her therapy. However, no matter how often I replayed our conversations, I just couldn't find anything that would explain her withdrawn state. For weeks I worked with her, encouraged her, tried to reach her. And what did I get in return, nothing! Until today that is."

"What happened today?"

"While I was massaging her, Denny opened one of her hands. A dozen or more pills fell onto the mattress."

"Pills? Like medication?"

"I thought so, hoped so, but I wasn't sure. Then I checked Denny's prescriptions."

Philip had that worried crease between his brows, "And?"

"Let's just say that those little red flags that let you know something's wrong — well, they were doing double time. Philip something is very wrong with Denny's medication. In fact, nothing seems right about it."

"Explain what you mean."

"After checking Denny's prescriptions, I found pills that were supposed to be in one bottle, were moved to another bottle, while other pills were removed all together and replaced with over-the-counter pain relievers. In other words, I had prescription bottles that didn't match the medications held inside."

"It could have been a pharmacy error."

"Maybe, but there's more."

Reaching into her pocket, Beth pulled several pills free, dropped them onto the island between them. She moved the little green pills into a pile.

"See these?"

"Yes."

"Do you know what they are?"

"No, I don't recognize them."

"Me either."

"What are you thinking, Beth?"

"Philip, I've been prescribing medications for more than a decade now. I know what's what in the world of psychiatric drugs. Particularly sedatives and antidepressants. I know which drugs are used to treat all sorts of mental disorders. I know them by name — I know them by sight."

"And?"

"And, I don't recognize these green pills. In fact, I haven't got a clue what they are. But, I know what they aren't. They are not the sedatives or antidepressants prescribed by Denny's doctor."

"So, what are you thinking?"

"I think someone has been drugging Denny."

"Who do you think would do that?"

"Her husband, Cliff Jameson."

"Why do you think he would drug his wife?"

"I don't know, but it is definitely a question that needs answering."

"Yeah, well here's another. What if you're wrong?"

"Then I'm screwed."

Darkness filled the house when Cliff pulled into the driveway. Instantly, he knew something was wrong, he didn't know what yet, but he knew something was terribly wrong. Nervous energy shot through him as he practically pulled the back door from its hinges. The nervous energy continued surging as he called through the silence.

"MOM!"

He waited a moment, then he tried again.

"MOM!"

Moving through the first floor, Cliff continued his yelling. Receiving only deafening silence in return, Cliff bounded up the stairs. Taking two at a time, he raced to the master bedroom, only to find it empty. In a fit of rage, Cliff pulled at Denny's bed, stripped it to its powder blue mattress before rushing back downstairs.

Retracing his steps, Cliff headed back toward the kitchen. Pacing the tiny room like a caged animal, Cliff tried to steady his frayed nerves before pulling the cordless phone from its base, and punching in his mother's number.

"Hello."

"Mom. Where's Denny? What's going on?"

"Cliff, I left a note on your desk in the study."

With that, the phone went dead.

Storming into a study, Cliff pulled Susan's note from his desk. His mother's feminine script seemed cheery enough, the words however, cut to the chase.

Dear Cliff,

I don't know how to begin this, except to say that I am sorry. I've been lying to you for a number of weeks now, and it seems as though I can no longer continue.

The lie concerns Beth. Beth isn't the niece of anyone I might know, and she doesn't give massages. Beth, Dr. Malone that is, is a therapist and she's been seeing Denny for a couple of months. I know you don't approve of therapy, and find little if any use in it, that's why I felt I needed to keep the truth from you.

Anyway, it appears that Denny is making progress and Dr. Malone thought it best to have Denny go spend time with her. Hopefully things will move right along with Denny's therapy, and then you and Denny can work things out.

I truly hope that happens, son. Just as I hope you can forgive me.

169

I'm heading out of town to spend time with your Aunt Paula. I'll call when I get back.
Love, Mom.

Balling up the note, Cliff tossed it onto the floor, then stomped it, over and over as he yelled.

"BULLSHIT! BULLSHIT! BULLSHIT! I'M BEING FED NOTHING BUT BULLSHIT!"

While he didn't know what for sure, he knew something was up. He knew it. He could feel it. Right down to his bones.

But, what?

Consumed with anger, Cliff replayed portions of Susan's note through his troubled mind.

Anyway, it appears that Denny is making progress and Dr. Malone thought it best to have Denny go spend time with her. Hopefully things will move right along with Denny's therapy, and then you and Denny can work things out.

"Denny's at Beth's? Working things out? We'll see about that you bitches!"

With only one thought, Cliff stormed out of his home.

Denny. I've got to get Denny back. At all costs!

~~ 40 ~~

Beth and Philip watched from a darkened window as Cliff sped onto their driveway, as he screeched to a halt, sending loose gravel and dirt flying in all directions. Huddled together, they watched as Cliff climbed their back steps, as he unleashed his fury against the tiny doorbell that sent foreboding chimes echoing through their home.

"Beth, we should call the police."

"No! We can't."

"For God's sake, why not?"

"BECAUSE HE IS THE POLICE."

"What?"

"He's a cop."

"A cop? You kidnapped a cop's wife? Are you insane?"

Finding only confusion where answers should be, Beth turned pleading eyes toward Philip. Eyes that begged him to believe in her, to help her, to support her, to love her, no matter what.

Despite the steady pounding coming from their backdoor, Philip found that he did believe her, knew that he would help her, support her, love her, no matter what.

Lifting Beth's chin, Philip pulled her close, looked deeply into her eyes that were wide with fear, turquoise eyes, beautiful eyes. With a quick kiss on her forehead, he took control. "Beth are you SURE he's been drugging Denny?"

"Are you asking if I can prove it, or if my instinct says it's so?"

"Instinct."

Without a moment's hesitation, Beth answered, "Yes, I'm sure he's been drugging Denny."

"Okay then, come on."

Pulling Beth along the upstairs hallway, Philip quickly checked in on Denny. Despite all the ruckus around them, he found their charge sleeping peacefully. Closing her door tight, Philip led his terrified wife toward the grand staircase.

"Where are we going?"

"We have company, Beth. We're going to answer the door."

"WHAT? ARE YOU CRAZY?"

"I'm afraid so!"

Pacing the back porch, Cliff quickly ran his options through his frenzied mind.

Kick the fucking door open. You know the alarm code, just disarm it. Find Denny. Find the bitch who took her. But, what if Denny's not even here? What if the bitch has already called the cops? What if she has company?

The what-ifs kept Cliff in check. After all, he didn't know where his wife was. He didn't know if she was even capable of communicating. Hell, he didn't know anything. He certainly didn't know if Denny had said anything to her bitch of a shrink. More importantly, he didn't know if the bitch had told someone else.

By the time Cliff saw lights being turned on throughout the first floor he was wild with anger and aggression. Seeing Beth walk toward him, wrapped in the protective embrace of a hulk of a man, sent him hurtling along an already ignited path. Turning toward the driveway, Cliff, for the first time, noticed a black BMW parked in front of Beth's Volvo.

Shit! She's not alone. Be careful, Cliffy. Really careful.

Philip moved into the mud room, keeping his wife tucked safely behind his massive body. Protected only by a half-glass, half-wood door, Philip faced the raving lunatic.

"Where's my wife?"

Speaking up from behind Philip, Beth didn't even bother trying to steady her trembling voice.

"She's someplace safe, Mr. Jameson."

"Where?"

"Mr. Jameson, I'd like you to leave my property. If you do not, I'll trigger the panic button on my security panel. Within minutes, this place will be surrounded by police."

"So! I am the police! Who do you think they are going to believe? I have cause to believe my invalid wife is here against her wishes, against mine."

"Mr. Jameson, I took Denny from your home because I suspect there's a problem with her medication."

Moving toward the door, Cliff began raising his arms with fists clenched. Without hesitation, Philip pulled a handgun from his pocket and aimed it directly at Cliff's head.

"Back up, or I'll blow a hole through your fucking head."

Of the three people standing there, Beth was quite sure she was the most surprised — by the gun, by the threat her husband made, and by what he said next.

"Mr. Jameson, let me cut to the chase. Dr. Malone believes that you have been drugging your wife. Purposefully attempting to cause her harm. I'm of the same opinion."

"Yeah, asshole? Well, your Dr. Malone there must not have any proof, or you'd have called the cops already."

Scooping several tiny green pills from her pocket, Beth held them out toward Cliff.

"What the fuck?" Cliff was completely taken by surprise.

"That's what I asked when these fell out of your wife's clenched hand this morning."

Again, Cliff moved toward the door, only to have his threat answered by the cocking of Philip's gun.

~~ 41 ~~

As though glued together, Beth and Philip watched as Cliff backed his car over their perfectly groomed garden. Several minutes passed before either of them moved a single muscle, several more before they spoke.

"Philip, the gun. Where did it come from?"

"My study."

"What? When?"

"This afternoon, when you were tending to Denny I took it from the wall safe."

"You mean it's yours?"

Philip simply nodded.

"And, you've had it in this house the whole time we've lived here?"

Another nod, and the beginnings of a smile.

"Good God, Philip. You know how I feel about guns. How could you?"

"Beth, imagine what might have happened without it tonight. And, I think we have more important things to discuss right now, don't you?"

Angrily pacing the mud room, Beth banged her toe on an antique bench that lined one wall. "Shit!"

"Beth darling, you're showing signs of stress."

"Oh yeah? Well how's this? Shit, shit, SHIT!"

"Very well done, my dear."

"Learned it all from you, love. Now, what was it exactly that you said to Mr. Jameson? Oh, I remember; 'Back up, or I'll blow a hole through your fucking head'. Yes, that's it. Verbatim, I believe."

Pulling the love of his life close, Philip felt her racing heart through their clothes. Felt it quicken when he planted a long, hard, deep kiss on her eager, waiting lips.

Looming over his wife, he whispered, "Desperate times, desperate measures, and all that."

Beth willingly followed Philip upstairs, stopping only momentarily to check on Denny. Finding her still fast asleep, Beth moved quickly down the hall toward her bedroom.

Closing the bedroom door behind Beth, Philip pressed his wife tight against it with his body, with his hips, with his lips. Pent up passion mixed with a deep love quickly sent Beth over the moon.

When Philip took Beth on top of their bed, it was new, exciting, and powerful.

Laying in his arms afterward, Beth knew she was safe. Safer than she had ever felt before, despite the danger that lurked somewhere outside their home.

Cliff dedicated several hours that night to trashing the home he had shared with Denny and his children. Hatred poured through him as his destruction mounted. Exhausted from the physical and emotional exertion, Cliff took to his study. A study that once offered him solitude from his family, from the world, and now offered only silence. Silence broken by the ticking of an anniversary clock that graced the corner of his desk. Reaching for the clock, Cliff tapped whatever energy he had left and whipped the tiny timepiece against the deep burgundy painted wall, shattering it into dozens of pieces. Amazingly, the mangled clock kept ticking. Tick, tick, ticking.

Focused on the repetitive sound, Cliff almost missed the ring of his phone a couple of minutes later. When he answered the wailing phone, he instantly wished he had not.

"Hey Cliff, it's Mike Carbone."

An uneasy feeling, one just south of panic, edged its way along Cliff's inner workings when he heard Carbone's voice.

Carbone? What does he want? Maybe Beth or the hulk with the gun called him. Shit!

"Mike, it's kind of late for calls isn't it?"

"Late? Really?"

"Yeah, well for those of us who work days anyway."

The newly appointed graveyard shift sergeant obliged Cliff with a good-sport chuckle.

He's in a good mood. This can't be too serious. Focus. Stay calm. Focus.

"Hey Cliff, you still there?"

"Yeah, what's up?"

"Well, your name came up during the investigation into Principal Reddy's shooting."

SHIT! Wait. Pay attention!

"My name? You sure?"

"Well, not your name, but you."

"Mike, it's late. Can we skip the riddles?"

"Sorry. Look Cliff, it seems that a waitress from a pizza shop over by the high school suddenly remembered seeing you the night of the shooting."

Shit!

"Really? Gosh I don't even remember. Oh, wait a minute, that's right Town Line Pizza. Sure, now that you mention it, I did stop in there that night. My mom likes their green pepper and pepperoni pizza."

"What time was that, Cliff?"

"Gosh Mike, I don't remember."

"The waitress said it was just before six."

"Okay, if she says so. I couldn't tell you though, things have been pretty screwed up around here, makes keeping track of time pretty difficult, you know what I mean?"

"Can only imagine. Sorry, man."

Move it along. Move the conversation away from the shooting. Don't ask anything. Don't look suspicious.

Unfortunately, Cliff didn't take his own advice.

"Hey Mike. The waitress, how did she suddenly remember me?"

"When you stopped in for a pizza, she said she recognized you from the high school dance a few weeks back."

"Humph. And all this time, I thought I was just a fly on the wall at those dances."

"You are. Seems she remembered you from the parking lot, not from the dance. From what she said, you caught her and her boyfriend doing the deed in his daddy's car."

No fucking way. Fuzzy pink sweater girl is the pizza shop waitress. What fucking luck. Shit fucking luck.

"Anyway Cliff, the reason I'm calling is I wondered if you noticed anything the night of the shooting. I mean you were near the right place at the right time. I know it's a long shot, but we're getting major heat over this case and we're no closer to solving it now then we were weeks ago."

Purely for effect, Cliff hesitated before answering. "Gosh Mike, I've got nothing."

"Yeah, well like I said, I figured it was a long-shot."

"I'll work on it Mike, get back to you if anything comes up."

"Yeah. Thanks."

Cliff hung up quickly, maybe too quickly. Too late to do anything about the phone call with Carbone, Cliff returned to the destruction of his home, sparing only Page and Preston's rooms from his fury.

~~ 42 ~~

After spending several hours wrestling with her feelings, Beth gave in to the strongest of those feelings, desire. Rolling on top of Philip, Beth gave herself, her whole self, to the only man she ever loved, as she took from him pleasures she had been denied for far too long. Rocking gently back and forth, Beth listened to her name being whispered over and over and over.

"Beth. Beth. Beth."

The sound of her name soothed her, moved her, branded her. She was his and he was hers. It was as simple as that. Simple. Just like their love. She knew that now. Their love was simple. Whatever complicated it before could be worked out. It would be worked out.

From some distant place, Beth heard her name again, louder, more urgent.

"Beth! Beth! Beth!"

Moved to tears, Beth felt Philip shudder beneath her just before her own love exploded.

Shrouded by a peaceful slumber, Beth wasn't sure who screamed, if anyone screamed at all. Weighed down by many layers of sleep, Beth lay perfectly still.

When the blood curdling scream resonated through the stillness again, she immediately realized it came from Denny's room. Pulling herself from Philip, Beth grabbed her terry robe and flew to Denny who was huddled in a corner, wild-eyed, and terrified. An almost indiscernible chant was repeated over and over.

"Cliff, no please don't. Please don't. Please don't."

Tender, soothing words filled the space between the two women.

"Denny. Denny. It's me, Beth. Are you alright?"

Within moments, Denny's chant was replaced with words Beth was sure she would never forget.

"Beth, it hurts so bad. I hurt so bad."

Crawling slowly on her hands and knees, Beth pulled Denny into her arms and cradled her in the dark for what seemed like hours. Sensing Philip's protective presence, Beth turned all her attention to the grief-stricken woman she had vowed to help.

The floodgate of tears finally dammed, Beth and Philip placed Denny back into bed, certain she would sleep the rest of the night. As it turned out, she was the only one who would.

From two until four that morning, Beth's phone rang forty-three times. Fatigued, concerned, pissed, Beth eventually proclaimed the painfully obvious. "It's Jameson, you know."

"I know."

"He's not going to give up."

"I know. What are you going to do?"

"Find out the truth."

"From?"

"Denny."

Unable to keep the image of the pathetic creature who slept in a room down the hall from his mind, Philip expressed his deeply rooted doubt.

"From Denny? I don't know, Beth."

"Well I do. Once we get all the shit he's given her out of her system, she'll be able to tell us exactly what happened to her. Then, we go to the police."

"That's gonna take time."

"So."

"So, what makes you think Jameson's gonna give you the time you need?"

"He doesn't have any choice. Denny's with us."

"Until he comes back to get her."

"You really think he'll come back?"

"Don't you?"

The wail of her phone answered that question for Beth and for Philip.

He will come!

~~ 43 ~~

Cliff would have called in sick Friday, if not for the phone call the night before from Mike Carbone.

If I don't show up for work, it might look suspicious. Someone might even stop by my house, and see the place torn to shit. No, no, I have no choice, I have to go to work. Denny and Beth will just have to wait! That bastard of a hulk will have to wait too.

On little to no sleep, Cliff headed toward the station. Then he decided to take the long route past 147 Hummingbird Lane. As expected, the black BMW and midnight blue Volvo were present and accounted for on the circle driveway.

Still inside, huh? Still inside with my wife?

Having no choice, Cliff buried the rage he felt and put on a calm exterior. An exterior he would show the world that day, but only because he had to.

But tomorrow ... well, we will just have to see about tomorrow ... when tomorrow comes.

Philip found Beth in the kitchen the next morning, busy making breakfast. That was the first thing he found odd that morning.

Taking the plate she offered him to the breakfast nook, Philip found a cup of coffee and a glass of freshly squeezed orange juice waiting for him. That, was the second thing he found odd that morning.

"How long have you been up?"

"An hour or so."

"And Denny? Is she up too?"

"Not yet."

Silence, a very thick silence, quickly filled the space between them. Silence that needed to be broken. Beth did the honors.

"Philip, now that a new day is here, I need to know if you've changed your mind. Changed your mind about helping me."

"Beth, I said I was in, so I'm in. There are still a lot of things that I need to know."

"Like?"

"Like why you don't just call the cops, and don't say it's because he's a cop, because that excuse only goes so far."

"I know."

"Then?"

"The pills I found yesterday, there is really no way I can prove Cliff gave them to Denny, without Denny's help."

"Why not?"

"He wasn't the only person responsible for her care."

"Who else took care of her?"

"Her mother-in-law."

"But, you're sure it wasn't the mother-in-law who drugged her."

"Yes, absolutely certain."

"Okay, then I'm sure the cops will come to the same conclusion. What's holding you back?"

"Me."

"I don't follow. What do you mean by that?"

"I took care of Denny, too. And I did so without her husband's knowledge or consent."

"What? How did that happen and why?"

"Denny's mother-in-law arranged the therapy sessions. Each Thursday she would sneak me into the house and if need be, she'd make up outlandish lies about who I was and why I was visiting Denny."

"Wait a minute; Jameson knew you visited Denny?"

"He came home unexpectedly on two occasions while I was there."

"And?"

"And, he's scum. I'm telling you Philip; he made my skin crawl. He's all flash on the outside, but inside he's nothing but a control freak."

"How do you know?"

"Right before Denny slipped into her catatonic state, she had given me some insight into her husband. It's the same old story, really. Guy impresses woman with his fascination with her, she thinks it's romantic that he's so smitten,

187

when all the while he's really covering the fact that he's a stalker.

"Then Mr. Wonderful makes the love of his life the center of his universe. However, in doing so, he becomes her entire world. Translation is isolation for the woman, of course.

"I was just beginning to get a picture from Denny of what her life with Jameson was like before she slipped beyond reach, but the broad strokes she had painted, certainly led me to my assessment of him."

"So, what you're telling me is that we're dealing with a control freak who spent countless weeks drugging his wife into a catatonic state?"

"Yes."

"We can add to that, the fact that we can't go to the police because you snuck into his home, administered therapy to his wife, without his consent. And I'm sure that the time you spent with Denny was private, right?"

"Yes."

"So, there were no witnesses to your sessions."

"Of course not."

"So, there's no one to say that you aren't the one who drugged Denny."

"No, counselor, there is not."

"Fool around if you want to Beth, but my being a lawyer just might come in handy for you one of these days."

Beth watched as Philip stormed through the mud room, and up the winding staircase. Alone in the kitchen, she felt the depths of reality as they slapped her silly.

~~ 44 ~~

When Beth entered the guest room that morning, she found that the previous day's events had taken a toll on Denny. Physically and emotionally. Curled into a fetal position, Denny stared blankly past Beth. Continued to stare off into space, as Beth addressed her, massaged her.

"Denny, I'm so glad you're here. We'll be able to do some really good work, Denny. Would you like that?"

Not expecting a response, but hoping for one nonetheless, Beth watched any for the slightest response. She received none.

"Denny, Cliff can't get to you. He won't harm you anymore. Do you understand that, Denny?"

Pulling away from Beth, Denny curled tighter into her fetal position.

"Denny, what is it? Is it Cliff?"

From behind her, Beth heard Philip's strong, baritone voice. "Beth, it's me. I think she's afraid of me."

His body filling the doorway, Beth knew was a sight that could intimidate just about anyone. Especially someone as fragile as Denny.

"Are you Denny? Are you afraid of Philip?"

Her eyes fixed on Philip, Denny offered a slight nod.

"Denny, Philip is my husband. He helped me get you here. Do you remember that?"

Your husband? Yes, I remember. He carried me from the car.

Again, Denny nodded.

"Denny, you're communicating. That's wonderful."

Motioning Philip to take a seat, Beth pressed on. "Denny, I'd like Philip to sit in on our session today, if that's all right with you."

Beth waited for a response. Waited as long as she could before continuing. "Denny, do you trust me? Trust that I have your best interest at heart?"

Yes, Beth. I do.

Denny nodded.

"Good, then we can begin if you're ready."

Denny nodded again.

"Denny, I'd like to go back and review some of the things we discussed before your setback."

You mean before Cliff drugged me practically into a coma?

Awareness flooded Denny's face telling Beth they were heading in the right direction.

"Okay Denny, when we last spoke, you were struggling with the pain of losing your children."

Pain and guilt.

"Do you remember that, Denny?"

A nod.

"Do you remember what else you were struggling with?"

Yes, guilt.

A nod.

"You had mentioned feelings of guilt. Guilt because you didn't get Page and Preston from school. Do you remember that Denny?"

I promised Page. I pinky swore that I would pick them up that day.

Waiting for a signal, any signal, Beth almost fainted when Denny looked at Beth, then at Philip and whispered, "I remember."

"What Denny? What do you remember?"

"I didn't pick Page and Pres up. They took the bus home. The bus was hit by a train. I broke my promise - and my children were killed."

"Do you think the accident was your fault?"

"No."

"Then why do you feel guilty, Denny?"

"Because I didn't pick them up, and if I had ..."

Denny didn't finish her thought; she didn't need to. Everyone in the room knew what she thought – what she felt. They all knew what she needed, too. She needed answers. She needed an answer to the question that plagued her.

192

Why didn't she pick her children up from school that day!

Certain that Denny knew the answer to that question on some level, Beth gently chipped away at the protective layers that kept the answer at bay.

"If you had picked the kids up that last day, they would still be alive? Is that what you're thinking, Denny?"

"Yes ... No."

"Which is it, Denny? Yes, or no?"

"Both.".

45

Beth's reward for her hard work, had come in the form of two words. Two little words. Yes, and no. Two very complex Little Words. Yes, and no.

"Can you explain what you mean by yes?"

"If I had picked them up, then of course they'd still be alive today. But ..."

"But? What?"

"But, there's more. I don't know what but there's more."

"Okay then, let's find out what else there is. Denny, I'd like you to relax, tune out the world around you, and listen only to my voice. Okay?"

"Okay."

"Denny. How do you feel?"

"Fine."

"Are you ready to talk about that last day?"

"Yes."

"Okay, Denny, tell me about that last day."

"From the beginning?"

"No. You already told me what happened at breakfast, and on the ride to school. So, why don't we jump ahead. Tell me what happened after you dropped the kids off that morning."

"I'd planned on washing the van, but it was raining, so I went directly home. Cliff was waiting for me."

"He wasn't working that day?"

"Yes, he was."

"Then why was he home?"

"He stopped for coffee."

"Did he stop for coffee often?"

"Yes."

"Okay. So you and Cliff had coffee. Then what?"

"He left."

"What did you do?"

Rapid eye movement beneath Denny's closed lids told Beth that Denny was replaying the day's events like a movie. A movie she'd eventually share with her audience.

"I went upstairs, stripped and remade Page and Preston's beds. I was about to do my bed, but I got this horrible headache, so I laid down. I must have fallen asleep."

"And then?"

"I can't remember."

"Can't? Or don't want to?"

"I don't know."

"Yes Denny, you do."

Encouraged by Beth's words, Denny collected her thoughts and her strength. "At some point, I woke up. Well, I sort of woke up."

"Tell me how you felt when you 'sort of woke up'."

"I felt tired, **really** tired. I remember trying to open my eyes, and while my brain was telling my eyes to open, they wouldn't."

"Then what?"

"Eventually, I opened my eyes. I tried to get up, because I knew I needed to get Page and Pres, but I couldn't get my head off the pillow. It felt like it weighed a thousand pounds. My arms and legs felt the same way. Heavy and awkward. Not quite paralyzed, but not functioning either."

"Okay, then what?"

"The bees came."

"Bees … like bumble bees?"

"Yes."

"Bees came into your room?"

"No. Into my head."

Forcing herself to weave carefully through the emotional minefield she and Denny were traveling, Beth took a moment to organize her thoughts.

Bees? Bees in her head. This is important … think … what could the bees mean? Okay, bees are bugs. Pests. Pests that sting. Cause pain. In some cases, kill.

Knowing there were countless opportunities for missteps along the way, Beth pressed on, hoping her next round of questioning would take them toward safer ground.

"Okay Denny, tell me about the bees.

46

"They interrupted my sleep."

"How?"

"They swarmed around, made it impossible for me to think."

"So, they bothered you?"

"Yes."

"Bugged you?"

"Yes."

"Did they hurt you? Sting you?"

"No, they just swarmed around, like they were angry."

"Okay, why were they angry?"

"Because I wouldn't get up."

"The bees were angry because you wouldn't get up?"

"Yes."

"Tell me more about the bees, Denny."

"Whenever they swarmed, I remembered I was supposed to pick up the kids from school. It was as though they bothered me so I'd check the clock."

"And did you check the clock?"

"Yes."

"Where was the clock?"

"On my nightstand."

"What did it say?"

Denny paused. Beth regrouped, and Philip remained still, perfectly still.

"It was one-twenty."

"A.M. or P.M.?

"One-twenty in the afternoon. I needed to leave by one-thirty to get the kids."

"And did you leave?"

"No. I couldn't."

"Why?"

"I couldn't get off the bed."

"Did you try?"

"Yes."

"What happened?"

"I pulled myself to the edge of the bed, but I collapsed back onto the mattress. I tried to get the phone."

"Why?"

"I wanted to call the school. I wanted them to keep Page and Pres there. I wanted to pick them up."

Giant tears ran along Denny's cheeks and pooled onto the pillow beneath her soft, blonde curls.

Half expecting Denny to pull herself into a fetal position, or to call it quits, Beth waited. Thankfully, she didn't have long to wait before Denny pulled herself together and continued on.

"When I reached for the phone, my hand shot away from me, like I had no control over it.

Anyway, I knocked my favorite picture of Page and Pres to the floor."

"The picture in the silver frame?"

"Yes."

"That's when it became broken?"

"Yes."

Another round of tears filled the depressing silence around them. When Denny composed herself, she resumed her tale of the tormenting bees.

"I tried to get the picture from the floor, but my head was throbbing so badly, it sent me flat against the bed again. I was at the mercy of the bees again, too."

"The bees; tell me about the bees."

"They kept swarming around. It was like they were chanting."

"Speaking? The bees were speaking?"

"No, not really. But whenever they swarmed, they made me think. First, about the time. It was like they needed me to know what time it was. Then, they were pushing me to realize that something was wrong. That I needed help. That's why I pulled the phone to me."

"The phone? You called someone?"

"I tried. I think I pushed the talk button and maybe even some numbers."

47

"Okay, you tried to dial the phone. Do you remember talking to anyone?"

"No."

"What do you remember?"

"Nothing."

"Nothing at all?"

"Nothing about the rest of that day."

"Okay, what's the first thing you remember after you tried to make that phone call?"

"Dirt being scattered over two shiny white boxes. Ashes to ashes – dust to dust."

Beth shot a horrified look toward Philip. Unfortunately, he had already hung his head, missing her silent plea for support.

Taking a moment to organize her thoughts, Beth was totally caught off guard when Denny broke the silence that engulfed them.

"Beth."

"Yes Denny."

"The way I felt that day."

"Yes."

"It wasn't the first time I'd felt that way."

"I know."

"And it wasn't the last time either."

"It wasn't?"

"No, there have been lots of times since then that I've felt **the exact same way**."

Beth knew what Denny was about to say, and she was pretty sure Philip knew as well, still, it came as a blow when Denny finally uttered the blood chilling words.

"And each and every time I felt that way, Cliff had given me a tiny green pill. Beth, I think Cliff must have given those pills to me countless other times as well. All the other times when I couldn't get the kids."

With that realization, Denny's floodgates burst.

So did Beth's.

So did Philip's.

Beth insisted that Denny eat something, then rest a while before resuming her session. It was during this time that Philip gave Beth the greatest gift he had ever given her.

"Beth."

"What?"

"The work you do — it's so terribly important. Beyond explanation or comprehension. Maybe that's why I never really understood how difficult it is for you to separate from your work. Why you **shouldn't** separate from your work."

Pulling Beth close, Philip bent to kiss her welcoming lips, stopped when he spotted the unmarked police car parked on their side street.

For over an hour, he'd kept his eyes trained on Beth's house. For all his efforts, he'd been rewarded with absolutely nothing. No Beth. No Denny. Nothing. Then, suddenly he was rewarded. And, his reward? Him and her. Talking. Embracing. Kissing.

When the hulk pulled away from Beth … his Beth … Cliff knew that they knew. They knew he was outside. Watching.

Yep, that's right. I'm watching. And, I've been watching. And, I'll continue watching. Until I'm ready to make my move.

~~ 48 ~~

Denny was waiting by the window when Beth and Philip returned an hour or so later.

"Cliff was out there."

It was Philip who responded. "Yes, we know."

"He knows I'm here."

"Did he see you?"

"Maybe. But, even if he didn't, he knows."

"How?"

"He knows everything."

Philip moved as close to Denny as he could while still leaving a generous amount of personal space between them.

Beth laughed to herself when she realized he had been paying attention when she'd mentioned things like 'personal space'. Realized more, too. Like how wonderfully caring he was when he addressed Denny.

"Denny. There's no doubt in my mind that your husband is guilty of drugging you. Under normal circumstances, I would recommend we go to the police, but …"

"But?"

"Well, from what I understand, **he is the police**."

"Yes."

"Police tend to protect their own, unless there's a mountain of evidence that says they can't. Right now, we don't have a mountain of evidence."

"What about the pills? And what about the fact that I will tell them he drugged me?"

The warning signs of Denny becoming unglued forced Beth into action.

"Denny. We have the pills, and we have you, but if Philip thinks we still don't have enough; then, we don't have enough."

"Evidence?"

"Yes."

"Philip knows about evidence?"

"Yes."

"Is he a cop, too?"

Beth took Denny's frail hands into her own. She gently rubbed warmth into them as she calmed her fears.

"No. No, he's an attorney. A defense attorney."

"Oh, he's scum?"

"Scum?"

"That's what Cliff has always called defense attorneys. He says he and the other cops work their asses off all day, every day, so pieces of shit scum like Philip can get the guilty off."

Philip's booming laugh startled Denny into a fit of laughter of her own.

When they resumed their session that afternoon, Denny was focused, and determined to move forward.

Beth however, was concerned about the mine-field that moving forward would lead them to. Still, she trudged on.

"Okay, Denny. Why don't you begin by telling me what you've learned so far."

"I've learned that I **didn't** get Page and Pres from school that last day because I **couldn't** get them. And, I **couldn't** get them because I'd been drugged by my husband."

"Okay, that's a great start. But, it's …"

"But, it's only the beginning. Beth, there's a lot more that I want to know. More that I hope I know."

"Like?"

"Like WHY? Why was Cliff drugging me?

"Okay, lets look at that — lets see what we come up with."

Denny turned her attention from Beth, toward Philip.

"Philip, in your experience, when a husband tries to cause harm, or actually causes harm to his wife, what does that mean?"

Philip knew where Denny was headed. Knew it was the most logical path to take. He also knew it was the most treacherous path. Receiving an approving nod from Beth, he acknowledged the worst.

"Nothing good, I'm afraid."

"Right, nothing good."

On a slippery slope, Beth jumped in to help guide Denny safely down.

"Denny, lets talk about your relationship with Cliff. What was it like?"

"It was a marriage. Most of it was good."

"Most?"

"Well, there were stressful times, but they usually revolved around Cliff and his job."

"His job? How so, Denny?"

"It was really important to Cliff that he be a true part of the police brotherhood. Sometimes I think he even changed who he was, or what he believed in, just so he could fit in better."

"Like?"

"Like when the kids started school. Cliff was adamant that they go to a private school. Well, private schools cost money. More money than our finances would handle. When Preston started school, money got tight. When Page started, tight went to lean. We were hurting financially. It caused a lot of stress on our relationship. But, not as much stress as my offering to get a part-time job caused. That offer, threw Cliff into a frenzy."

"He didn't want you to work?"

"He didn't want me to **have** to work. To **have** to supplement his income. He took the role of breadwinner seriously. It was his job to earn a living for his family. If his day job didn't cover our expenses, then he would supplement the family income by taking on more work. That's when he began his steady career at extra pay jobs."

Philip chimed in on the subject of extra pay jobs. "The working cop's part-time jobs?"

"Right. Good pay, easy work."

"Did Cliff pull a lot of extra pay jobs?"

"Not at first, but once he got his foot in the door, his charm and wit must have won the desk sergeant over. Before you knew it, he was out at least three times a week. Sometimes the weekends too."

"So, he solved your money problems, and he liked the work."

"He liked some better than others, but overall, I'd have to say he liked the work."

"What were his favorite extra pay jobs?"

"High school stuff. Dances, sporting events, graduations. He would do just about anything to land a high school gig.""

When the discussion of extra pay jobs was over, Beth took the lead once again. Comfortable on the fluffy guest room bed, Denny willingly followed that lead.

"Denny, how was Cliff with Page and Preston?"

"Cliff's a really great dad. Attentive to their needs and wants. Very involved in their school work and outside interests. He adores them. They adore him, too."

Denny referring to her children in the present tense wasn't lost on Beth, on Philip, or on Denny.

"I mean, he adored them, and they adored him, too."

The tender memories Denny shared of Cliff with their children, were in such contrast to the picture Beth had conjured in her mind. A mind that found it difficult, if not impossible, to connect the dots of who Cliff Jamison really was.

"Denny, you said you had missed appointments with your kids before that last day. Your mother-in-law said that there were changes in you changes that started about 6 months before the accident. As a matter of fact, Susan said Page had noticed changes in your behavior. That she had even mentioned it to Susan."

"She did? Page said something to Susan? About me?"

"Yes."

"What? What did she say?"

Having opened the can of worms, Beth moved through the slimy mess as quickly, and as painlessly as possible.

"Page said you were different."

"Different. Yes, Page would have noticed, she would have said something to Susan about it, too. Different. Yes, I suppose I was different."

Giant tears dropped onto Denny's folded hands. Hands that once held, protected, and nurtured her children. Children who were taken away, stripped from her life. Children who were denied the opportunity to be with their mother. They're true, real, honest mother. Not the one created by their father and his hideous world of drugs.

The more Denny thought about her last months with her children the more she cried. For herself, for her daughter, for her son. But most of her tears were shed because her children thought she was different.

Watching Denny ride her anguish to the lowest of lows, tore at Beth's heartstrings. Strings tenderly woven around her love for Philip. Strings that she hoped would prove strong enough to withstand their current state.

As if reading her mind, her thoughts, her heart, Philip mouthed the words, I love you. With those three little words, Beth felt her heartstrings tighten with joy.

Turning her attention back to Denny, Beth broached the most pressing subject of all. "Denny, during those last 6 months, did anything change between you and Cliff?"

"Other than his drugging me?"

"Yes."

Consumed by a fit of laughter, Denny looked Beth squarely in the eye and fessed up. "God, Beth! Cliff was going out practically every night. The only time he and I spent together was when he came home in the mornings for coffee. I'm certain now, that he was having an affair. But do you think I picked up on any of the signs. Nooo. Not me."

Beth knew what Denny meant by signs, but she wanted Denny to be the one to put the idea out there. She wanted Denny to drop the proverbial bomb, so she could help with the inevitable fallout.

"Signs?"

"That that he was cheating on me, having an affair. The signs were there, Beth, I just chose to ignore them. Just like I ignored what was happening to me."

"Did you? Ignore what was happening to you?"

After a thoughtful moment, Denny's surprised them all. "No. I guess I knew something was wrong. At first, I thought it was something little, like fatigue. After a while, I thought it was something big, maybe life-threatening. I remember lying awake some nights, panicked over the thought of dying and leaving my kids behind. I never once thought I would be the one left behind. Never once."

~~ 50 ~~

Minutes, shrouded in silence, passed without so much as a word, a glance, a thought being shared. Still, there was so much communicating going on, that Beth had difficulty deciding which direction to head next.

Thankfully, Denny took care of that for her.

"Beth, Cliff told me it was my fault that the kids died."

"When?"

"I'm not sure exactly, but I think it was pretty recently. Yes, recently, very recently."

"How do you know?"

"Well, it was after he started giving me the green pills."

"The pills. Denny, what can you tell me about the pills?"

"After the funeral, Cliff stayed with me around the clock. He was actually very kind, supportive, almost loving. When he went back to work, things changed. He changed."

"How?"

"I don't know, but his actions and his words, they didn't seem to ring true. On the outside he seemed caring, attentive, devoted, but there was a definite edge. At least I felt there was an edge."

"And the pills?"

"Oh, right. After Dr. Valez came to see me, Cliff started giving me pills first there were white oval shaped pills. Cliff said they were sedatives but they didn't make me sleepy. They made me feel better though."

"How so?"

"I'd been in bed for quite a while, I was stiff all over, and my head throbbed constantly. The white oval pills seem to alleviate my aches and pains."

Beth shot Philip a knowing glance, a glance Denny picked right up on.

"Beth, you told Susan the white oval pills were over the counter pain relievers."

"Yes, that's right."

"I thought they were sedatives."

"Why did you think that?"

"Because that's what Cliff told me they were."

"And the shiny purple pills, what did Cliff tell you they were?"

"Antidepressants."

"Do you remember how you felt after taking a purple pill?"

"Tired. Very tired."

"That's because they are the sedatives Dr. Valez prescribed for you."

"So, the green pills, are they the antidepressants Dr. Valez prescribed?"

"No."

"What are they?"

"I haven't the faintest idea."

"Well, whatever they are, they're God awful."

"Why, how do they make you feel?"

"Well, for one thing, they have an almost paralyzing effect. While that's bad enough, it's not nearly as bad as living through the nightmares those horrible little pills cause."

"Nightmares?"

"No, what those things give you are worse than nightmares. They're more like Stephen King-mares."

Beth found the reference to Stephen King amusing and insightful. The look on Philip's face said he did as well. The look on Denny's face however, said she found it anything but amusing.

The blare of a car's horn jolted them back to reality.

"Oh, God. It's Cliff."

Confirming Denny's fears when he looked to the street below, Philip motioned for Beth to keep Denny away from the window.

Sitting on the edge of the bed, her arm draped protectively around Denny, Beth asked Philip for a play-by-play.

"What's he doing?"

"Letting us know he's still around, that he's not giving up."

"How?"

"Well, right now he's leaning against his car waving to me."

"Waving?"

"Yup."

"He can see you?"

"Better than I can see him, I'm afraid."

"Why?"

"Because he's using a set of binoculars."

"You're kidding, right?"

It was Denny who responded to Beth's remark. "No, I'm afraid he's not."

~~ 51 ~~

After pulling his binoculars from his bag, Cliff made a quick assessment of Beth's house.

Kitchen - empty.

Livingroom - empty.

Front porch - empty

Upstairs bathroom - empty.

Empty - Empty - Empty.

Low on time, Cliff reached in through the car window, and laid on the horn. Then he waited. In under a minute, Beth's hulk filled the second-floor window.

Bingo!

Raising his binoculars, Cliff searched past the hulk, hoping for a glimpse of her. Ignoring his father's sage advice about stalking prey, Cliff lifted his arm toward the hulk and shot a hearty wave.

That's right asshole, I'm back! And I'll keep coming back until I have Denny, and Beth.

Philip let Beth and Denny know what their stalker was up to before moving from the window.

"He's gone."

"For now. He'll be back you know."

"Yes, Denny, I know."

"Soon."

"Yes, soon."

"Then we'd better get back to work."

Beth jumped right in. "Denny, you said the green pills gave you terrible nightmares."

Denny shuddered her response. "Yes."

"Did you have a nightmare every time Cliff gave you a green pill?"

"No, I'm not sure, but I think I had nightmares when he gave me a green pill, maybe after he'd given me some other kind of drug."

"What do you mean?"

"Cliff was adamant about my eating things he prepared for me, and was particularly insistent about my eating his soup. Unfortunately, soup was on the menu most afternoons. So, if Susan fed me soup, and Cliff followed up with a green pill, I would be plagued with nightmares that evening."

"The nightmares. Tell me about the nightmares."

"Almost all of them were about Page and Pres, about our last day together. When the dreams came to me, they were easy, comforting, and pleasant. Very much like the time we spent together that morning; and then until I dropped the kids off at school. The easy flow of things seemed to lull me into a sense of security, almost made me feel that there would be a different end to the dreams. A different end to reality. So, the dreams were welcome - in the beginning that is."

"And then?"

"Then after I dropped the kids off at school things would spiral downward pretty fast."

Denny pulled a long, slow, deep breath before continuing.

"As I traveled along that last day, my anxiety level increased so much so, that by the time I made it to my bedroom, I was wired. Inside and out."

"Denny, can you explain what you mean by inside and out?"

"Inside, tension and anxiety seem to dance along every fiber of my being. When I would wake in the morning, I'd be exhausted. Sometimes, every muscle in my body screamed in pain."

"You're probably right about your physical experiences, Denny. After all, it's not only the mind that holds on to our memories, our bodies do as well. They actually work in unison, not only during the time of a traumatic event, but afterward as well."

~~ 52 ~~

Hoping she hadn't broken Denny's momentum with her psych 101 lesson, Beth urged Denny to continue. Thankfully, Denny had no trouble picking up where she had left off.

"Anyway, when the bedroom memories hit, they hit hard. Any sense of peace I had was replaced with a sense of urgency, doom, dread. But most of all, I was tormented by words."

"Words?"

"Tormenting, taunting words that kept tumbling over and over in my head."

"The words, Denny. Can you focus on the words?"

"They were about that last day. Over and over I heard the words, 'last day', 'their last day' ... Page and Pres don't get on the bus ... please ... I need to get up ... time ... what time is it? One-twenty ... call the school ... tell them to have Page and Pres wait ... tell them not to take the bus ... I'll be there ... I promised ... something's wrong ... I need help ... what's wrong with me?

"Over and over, the words tormented me. At first, it seemed like I was watching, and starring in, a videotaped version of that last day. Everything was the same. The paralyzed feeling, the lethargy. Even the room was the same. Bright light that streamed through the bedroom windows that day, shown brightly on my nightmares, too. And the picture of Page and Pres…"

"Yes."

"Well, when the dream began, when I first turned toward the clock to see what time it was, the picture was fine. Perfect, not broken. So was the glass that Page and Pres smiled through. But, every time I looked at the picture, there were more and more cracks."

Squeezing her eyes closed, Denny released whatever tears she had left.

Giving Denny her moment of grief, Beth turned toward Philip, saw so many things written on his face. Sadness and concern for Denny; pride and encouragement for her.

Taking hold of that encouragement, Beth moved Denny forward.

"Okay, Denny. You said a minute ago that everything seemed the same when your nightmares began. Does that mean that they changed along the way?"

"Yes."

"How?"

"When the picture frame first fell in my dream, it fell to the bedroom floor. Just like it did when I knocked it from the nightstand that day. But, by the end of my nightmare I was no longer in my bedroom, and the picture no longer fell to my bedroom floor."

"Can you remember where you were at the end of your dreams?"

"Yes. I was in the woods."

"Woods? Like in a forest?"

"Sort of. I was in the woods that circle Lake Chumgawanga."

"Chumgawanga? The lake over in Danbury?"

"Yes."

"How do you know it was that lake?"

"I've been there before. It was actually one of the first places Cliff took me when we began dating. He loved it there, so we went dozens of times. In no time at all, it became our place. Whenever we went, we would spend the whole day. We would hike the woods for hours, eventually making our way to the water for a picnic. After we ate, we would swim for a while, then would make love on the sandy shore. I think that's where Preston was conceived."

"So, Cliff wasn't the only one who liked Lake Chumgawanga."

"Liked. It's interesting that you used the past tense of like."

"Really? Why?"

"Because we all **liked** it there. Cliff, his dad, his mom, me. **Liked** it until the accident, that is."

"Accident?"

"Hunting accident. Cliff's dad was killed in the woods surrounding the lake just after Pres was born. I don't think any of us have been back there since."

"But that's where the nightmares took you."

"Yes."

"Is there a connection of some sort?"

"I've had a lot of time to think about that. So far, I haven't come up with anything."

"Maybe if we keep moving forward. Okay?"

Denny pulled another deep breath before nodding.

"Denny, you're in the woods. Tell me about the picture of Page and Preston."

"The picture was leading me through the woods toward the lake. With every step I took, the picture remained just beyond my grasp, and every time I tried to reach it, I would tumble to the forest floor. Whenever I fell, the picture frame would tumble to the ground as well. Sometimes it would fall so close that I was sure I'd be able to reach it. But when I would try, it would rise, and then begin to move forward again.

"Eventually, the frame led me to a cliff that overlooks the east end of the lake. When we were kids, we used to jump from the cliff into the lake below. The dangers of the rocky ledge and the huge rocks just below the surface of the water thrilled us to no end. I can't imagine doing it now, but back then ..."

"Denny, the picture. Tell me about the picture."

"Right, the picture. When I made it to the top of the cliff, the picture was there, waiting for me.

Suspended above the water just beyond my reach. Heavily cracked glass practically obscured Page and Preston's faces. Their faces by this point were animated. Page and Pres were alive behind the cracked glass of that silver frame.

"Alive, and I had to save them.

"Instinctively, I moved toward the edge and reached out as far as I could without going over. Hope sprang eternal when my fingers grazed the picture. That hope was dashed when the contact caused the frame to bob up and down. Desperate to save the kids, I lean farther out over the water, reaching one last time for the frame. Unfortunately, someone pushed me from behind. Pushed me and then pulled.

"The forward motion of my body caught me so off guard that my hand jerked forward, striking the picture. The force of that contact caused the frame to hurdle forward, then downward. By the time the frame reached the water, both Page and Preston had been freed from behind the cracked glass.

"For what seemed like hours, they hurtled silently toward their deaths. Just before they plunged into the water, they screamed my name."

53

There were no words spoken for several minutes. When Denny finally found words, she surprised her audience once again.

"Beth, I've spent countless hours thinking about my nightmares, trying to figure out what they mean."

"What did you come up with?"

"Probably just obvious stuff."

"Like?"

"When I tried to reach the frame, and I couldn't, well, the feelings I had were the same as when I couldn't get off the bed that day.

"And the cracked glass in the silver picture frame. When the picture fell onto the bedroom floor, the glass that protected Page and Pres broke just a little. But in my dreams, by the time I'd reached the cliff, the point of no return, the glass in the frame was shattered.

"Just as I imagine, the windows of the bus were shattered when it was hit by the train.

"Beth, when Page and Pres broke free from the frame, and called my name just before hitting the water? Well in my dream, they died together, just like in real life. While I have no way of knowing if Page and Pres knew they were going to die, I'm pretty sure if they did, I'd be the first, and maybe the only thought they would have before the train hit them. Maybe they even called out for me."

The momentum of Denny's sobs not only wracked her tiny body, but Beth's as well as she gently rocked Denny back and forth. For more than an hour, Beth held onto Denny, helplessly listening to her heart wrenching sobs. When Denny was ready to emerge from her own personal hell, she pulled free from Beth's embrace, and whispered her name.

"Beth"

"Yes, Denny?"

"What do you think?"

"About?"

"About my dreams? And what I think they might mean?"

"I think they mean exactly what you said."

"Me too. Want to know what else I think?"

"If you're up to it, sure."

"When I was trying to reach the frame — right before it plunged into the water — someone pushed, then pulled me from behind."

"Yes."

"Do you remember where I was standing when that happened?"

"On the cliff overlooking the lake."

"Yes. ON THE CLIFF. The cliff that someone tried to push me off; the cliff that would have killed me had I fallen off. But I didn't fall, I didn't die. My children died, though. Why? Because I wasn't able to protect them. And what couldn't I protect them from?"

"The cliff?"

"No, not **the** cliff. CLIFF!"

54

"Denny, what are you saying?"

"CLIFF drugged me, for months. I know that now, but what I don't know is why. Why did he drug me? Let's say he drugged me because he wanted to kill me. ME. Not Page. Not Pres. I'm sure that was his plan. But, what happened? Something terrible happened. My children were killed in a freak accident. Did Cliff want that to happen? Absolutely not.

"Just like in my dreams, Cliff didn't want the picture frame that held his children to fall off the cliff into the lake. No, he wanted me to fall. He wanted me to die. I think my dreams are telling me that. Confirming that. Beth, what do you think?"

"I think you're amazing."

"I'm right, too. I mean why else would I be standing on the edge of a CLIFF, and married to a man named CLIFF, both of them ready, willing and able to cause my death, unless there's a connection?"

Unable to remain silent a moment longer, Philip answered Denny's rhetorical question.

"There's a connection, Denny. Now all we have to do is get some proof. Some irrefutable proof.

"Proof. Yes, proof."

Uttering those words, Denny lay her head against her pillow, and immediately fell into a deep sleep.

Busying herself with cups of tea, Beth half-listened as Philip retrieved messages from their answering machine.

"Twenty-seven hang ups," he announced as he sipped his tea.

"Any messages?"

"Nothing that can't keep."

"You know what I mean, Philip. Are there any messages from Cliff Jameson?"

"Besides the hang-ups?"

"Yes."

"Yes."

"What did he say?"

"Nothing, just a maniacal laugh."

"God, he's sick."

"Yes, doctor. I do believe you're right."

"Philip."

"Beth."

The way he said her name let her know how frustrated he was with the situation.

"Look, Philip. Maybe Jameson's like the wolf in the *Three Little Pigs*. You know, lots of huffing and puffing, but not much else."

"For God's sake, Beth. The man drugged his wife, probably planned to kill her. Add to that, the unfortunate deaths of his children and the fact that you kidnapped his wife. What does that add up to? Too much for your huffing and puffing theory, that's what!"

"It wasn't a theory, Philip. More like wishful thinking."

"I know. But wishing's not going to make it so. Look Beth, we've got a problem on our hands; a real problem."

"I know."

"Okay, do you also know that Jameson means business. He's not going to make a little noise, then go away. He's gonna come back, again and again, until he gets what he wants."

"Maybe we should call the police."

"There's no maybe about it. We **should** call. We're in way over our heads on this. But we can't call. Not yet anyway."

"Why not?"

"Look, if Jameson can talk himself out of the corners we think we've backed him into, and the cops believe him instead of us, he wins."

"This isn't a game, Philip."

"Yes Beth, it is. And the sooner we all realize that, the better."

"What do you mean?"

"Think of this as a game of chess. Jameson made his move — he drugged Denny.

"Denny made her move — she gave you the pills.

"You made your move — you kidnapped Denny.

"Jameson made his next move — he came here to get his wife back.

"We made our move — we forced him away with the threat of bodily harm.

"As we speak, Jameson's making his next move."

"How?"

"He's taunting us — phone calls, visits, threats."

"So, what should our next move be?"

"Nothing."

"Nothing? Really?"

"Well, not exactly nothing. We've already started a move that Jameson knows nothing about."

"What do you mean?"

"We started learning about our enemy. Denny's been our greatest asset in that. So, the behind the scenes move of ours might just be the most important move we make."

"Okay, I see your point. It's a game. So what's next?"

"Some more behind the scenes maneuvering. By Jameson, and by us. Eventually, Jameson's gonna have to make another move."

"And until then?"

"We protect our queen so that when the time comes, we can play her."

The house was dark when Cliff pulled into the driveway a little before eight. Remained dark as he made his way through the litter of memories he made the night before. Grabbing a pillow from the heap of a mattress that once held the heap of his wife, Cliff made his way back down the hall, toward his children's rooms. Tossing the pillow onto the floor between Page and Preston's rooms, Cliff forced himself to think, to plan, before sleep took him hostage.

After tucking Denny into bed that night, Philip and Beth retired to their bedroom to begin their wait for Jameson.

"Do you think he's out there?"

"I don't know. Maybe."

"But, he'll come tonight? Right?"

"Maybe."

"Is the security system on?"

"Yes."

"So, if he tries to get in, the alarm will go off, the cops will come and get him for breaking and entering. Right?"

"Right."

"That's when we tell everything else we know, right?"

"Right."

"He knows we have a security system. Do you think he'll be stupid enough to try to break in?"

"I don't know."

Looking out over her darkened property, Beth's face clearly showed the stress of the situation. Internally, that stress was compounded by the effects of a disappointingly unproductive afternoon with Denny.

"Philip."

"Yes."

"This afternoon with Denny, she was hunting something. Something in her mind. Something big, about that last day."

"I know. I felt she was close to finding it."

"Maybe she will find what is eluding her tomorrow. I hope she finds it."

Beth could almost hear sleep's tender voice as it called out to her husband. Surrendering her love to slumber, Beth silently pressed her face against the window, and tried hard to calm the storm of thoughts that danced in her head. Nagging, disturbing thoughts. When all was said and done, Beth accepted the one thought that refused to die. Accepted it as a friend, and ally, a warning. And that thought?

There's no rest for the wicked.

A fortified, and dangerously determined Cliff pulled himself from the floor a little before four am. Just as he'd pulled himself from bed countless times before for the hunting trips he took with his father.

Hunting. Yep. Time to go hunting.

As though preparing the hunter, the warrior in him, Cliff quickly changed clothes, gathered his two favorite weapons from the study's safe, and reviewed his plan. His game plan. After all, this was a game — *the game to end all games*.

When the hunter was ready, he left his home in search of his prey.

~~ 56 ~~

Cliff drove past Beth's house three times before parking his car and backtracking on foot. Having filled the silent trip with a little ditty that he hummed over and over, he now found it difficult to push the melodic tune from his head. His inability to remember the words to the tune that tumbled through his mind like a dusty old weed, almost sent him over the edge. Filling the vast wasteland of his head with several, La La La's, Cliff continued hunting the words that stubbornly remained on the fringes of his memory.

"La, la la. Hmm, hmm, hmm. La, la la."

Having traveled the route to his intended's numerous times, he had no trouble finding his way along the darken streets, lighted only by quaint antique gas lamps, or through perfectly manicured yards protected by only decorative fences that declared one property line from the next. Hell, even the laurel and holly bushes that stood guard over Beth's terrain didn't bother trying to keep him from his wife, or from his Beth.

"La, la la. Hmm, hmm, hmm. La, la la."

Anxious about what lay ahead, Cliff forced himself to focus on the tune. Soon little snippets came flooding back, not enough to satisfy him fully, but enough to let him know he was sniffing in the right direction.

"Police. Sting. Early, or maybe mid-eighties. La, la, la. Breath you take. La, la la. Claim you stake. Bond you break."

BINGO!

"I'll be watching you. Yup, watching you, hunting you, having you."

Blessed by a moonless night, Cliff inched his way toward the main house. Carefully checking his options, he quickly decided the back door was the easiest route of entry. Without so much as a whisper, Cliff popped the lock, and punched in Beth's security code, hoping all the while it would be the same code as the one for the tiny brick building.

It was.

Pleased when the red light turned green, Cliff repeated the cheery little poem he recited once before.

"8563. See Beth ... I came to thee."

The hair on the back of Philip's neck announced danger long before he opened his eyes. Holding Beth tightly in his arms, Philip used the stillness of the night to beckon his senses to life. Something was up. He knew it. He felt it. He feared it.

Grabbing his gun from the nightstand, Philip pulled himself free of Beth's embrace and went in search of whatever it was that raised his hackles.

Comforted by the steady red light that greeted him from the security panel at the bottom of the master staircase, Philip began retracing his steps toward his bedroom. Froze in place when he felt the muzzle of a gun pressed tightly against his back.

Cliff whispered into Philip's ear the same words Philip had previously used on Cliff. "Back up, or I'll blow a hole through your fucking head."

Moving from the bottom step, Philip inched along a path Cliff cut for him.

"Keep heading down the hall, toward the mudroom."

As they passed by the security panel, Cliff raised his hand, and deftly punched in Beth's code. With no fanfare whatsoever, the steady beam of light turned from red to green.

"Open the door."

"The security code. How did you get the code?"

"Open the fucking door."

As soon as Philip opened the door, Cliff punched in the security code again, and just like that, the light went from green to red.

Jabbing his gun deeply into Philip's back, Cliff forced him to move just far enough beyond the door. Whipped almost into a frenzy, Cliff pulled the door closed behind them before tormenting his prisoner. "It must be a relief knowing the girls will be nice and safe until I get back. Is it?"

"Listen Jameson."

"Shut the fuck up and move."

"Where?"

"The brick building."

Swallowed by the darkness around them, Philip gladly, willingly led his captor away from the women he'd vowed to protect. Turning his attention away from the gun pressed tightly into the flesh of his left shoulder blade, and toward the gun that flopped freely against his thigh, Philip quickly devised a plan. A plan that relied heavily on the gun in his bathrobe pocket.

"Okay asshole, open the door."

"I don't have the keys."

"I know, but I do."

Reaching into his pocket, Cliff pulled Beth's keys free, jingled them in Philip's face. "For future reference, you really shouldn't leave your keys out where just anyone can find them. They're just way to important. Don't you think?"

Cliff's words slammed around Philip's head.

*For future reference ... future reference. Future. Will there be a future? Only if you can get to your gun. You **need** to get to your gun!*

Nudging Philip forward, Cliff pressed his body tight against Philip's, wedging him against the brick building. "Give me your gun."

"What gun?"

"The fucking gun in your pocket. The one digging into my fucking thigh. That fucking gun, asshole."

Philip dragged his arm along the rough brick before sliding his hand into his bathrobe pocket.

"Hand it to me by the barrel."

Trading Philip's gun for Beth's keys, Cliff laughed his next instruction. "Unlock the door. Good, now open it."

Moving all his weight onto the door, Philip quickly turned the handle, sending the door flying open, and the men flying against the inside far wall. Using the momentum of his hitting the wall, Philip swung back toward Cliff, only to feel the butt of Cliff's gun as it sliced through his cheekbone, and the blunt force of his foot as it kicked the wind from his lungs. Reeling back against the wall, Philip watched as Cliff deftly plugged Beth's security code into the panel, seconds before the alarm sounded.

"Nice try, asshole. Maybe better luck next time, huh?"

Without so much as a warning and with cat-like precision, Cliff turned toward Philip. Placed the gun against his chest, and pulled the trigger.

~~ 57 ~~

Philip's body jerked back against the wall as thousands of volts of electricity shot through him. Before he hit the floor, his mind registered what had happened.

Stun gun.

Unable to move, barely able to breathe, Philip lay in a heap at Cliff's feet, watched helplessly as Cliff gazed lovingly at his weapon of choice.

"Pretty nice, huh? It's an Extreme XL Stun Gun. Packs one hell of a punch, don't you think? Think — that's the beauty of a stun gun, it takes your enemy down, keeps them down, but doesn't fuck with his mind. Nope, the mind keeps on working. Makes my game so much more interesting, right?"

Using the only thing available to him, Philip tried to wrap his brain around the situation at hand. Concentrating on Cliff's words, Philip feared what was in store for him, but not nearly as much as he feared what was in store for the women he promised to protect.

"So, asshole. How did it feel when the 50,000 volts shot through you? What's that? You can't remember? Well, how about we give it another try!"

Helpless to move, Philip lay waiting for another shock to his system. When Cliff delivered it, Philip wasn't sure whether he should pray for life or death. So, he didn't pray at all.

Startled awake, Beth reached next to her for comfort, for safety, for love. Finding only cold, empty sheets, Beth feared she had been abandoned. Feared that she would be alone, and might be alone for quite some time.

Stepping into her slippers, Beth quickly made her way toward Denny's room. Finding her guest sleeping peacefully, she headed out in search of her husband. By the time she reached the kitchen, it was perfectly clear where Philip was.

"My office?"

Cutting through the night like a steel blade, bright light poured from every room of the small brick building.

"What on earth?"

After punching a series of numbers into the security pad, Beth dashed across the driveway and into the little building without so much as a single thought of Cliff Jameson.

Pushing the office door open, Beth was greeted by her husband's limp body.

"Philip!"

Before making it to her husband's side, Beth felt herself being jerked upward and backward as though she were nothing more than a rag doll. Felt a gasp of air being pushed from her lungs as her body was hurled and then pinned against her office wall.

"Hello, Beth."

"You? How? What have you done to my husband?"

"Not much. Not yet anyway. But, the party is just getting started."

"What do you want?"

"Aw, come on Beth. What do you think I want?"

"Denny, but she's not here."

"Really?"

"No."

"Then where is she?"

Silence had a death like grip over Beth, even when Cliff jammed the end of a gun against her breast, she remained silent. It was only when Cliff took a step toward Philip, that she gave in.

"No, don't. Please. She's here. Well, not here, but in the house."

"I know."

Her composure nearly lost; Beth fought to stem the river of tears that streamed down her face.

"Aw, what's the matter Beth? You seem sad. Are you sad, Beth? Or tense, yes that's it, you seem tense. Maybe you need a massage.

Would you like that Beth? Of course you would, after all you're a masseuse right?"

Desperate to distance herself from a madman, Beth tried to move away from Cliff. Clamping onto her wrist until she yelped in pain, Cliff cajoled, "Oh Beth, I'm sorry. Did I hurt you? I didn't mean to, really. As a matter of fact, hurting you is the last thing on my mind. No, no Beth, I'm not going to hurt you. Your husband maybe. But not you."

Twisting her arm behind her back, Cliff pulled her toward him. His erection obvious to them both.

Moving the only part of her body that she could, Beth dropped her head, only to feel it being pulled back by her hair.

"Don't resist me, Beth. It will only make things worse. For you and for him."

"Please don't hurt him."

"Well, in order for you and me to have a little fun I'm going to have to give him one more jolt."

"No, please don't."

"Don't worry, it won't kill him. But when he hears how much fun you and I are having, he'll probably wish it had."

After delivering three 'stunning' shots into her husband, Cliff tossed a set of handcuffs toward Beth.

"Cuff him."

"What?"

"Put one cuff on his wrist, the other through the handle on that file drawer."

Afraid to move, afraid not to move, Beth stared into Philip's eyes. Desperate for a sign of encouragement, a sign that he was still with her, that he still loved her, Beth reached out to Philip with her thoughts, her heart, her prayers. Only to have her hopes dashed by the tap on her shoulder from the tip of Cliff's gun.

"Cuff him!"

Tightening the cuff around Philip's wrist, Beth gingerly felt for a pulse. Relief flooded through her when the faintest flutter kissed her fingertips, then relief was replaced with terror when she heard Cliff's words.

"Okay, let's go."

"Where?"

"The backroom."

"Why?"

"I'm gonna let you 'shrink me' doc."

"You're sick."

"Well, you should know."

Tucking the stun gun into the waistband of his jeans, Cliff lunged toward Beth. Hitting her with the full weight of him, Beth found herself pressed between her rock and a hard place. Between a wall and a maniac.

Each turn of her head, Beth managed to avoid the slobbering kiss of her captor; managed to move within reach of the security systems panic button as well.

Pulling her hair downward, Cliff lifted Beth's face close to his and calmly warned, "Don't even try. If you do, I'll blow his brains out, and then yours.

Grabbing her wrists, Cliff clamped tight before dragging her from the front office, toward the backroom.

Broken, jagged ribs pushed against his lungs while the cuffs around his wrist pinched off the circulation. Tiny stun gun burns on his skin blistered and stung and blood trickled from a gash on the back of his head. Still, nothing hurt quite so much as what he had seen Cliff do to Beth, or what he knew he was about to do to her in that back room.

Beth was forced to watch as Cliff removed his jacket, as he folded it neatly, as he placed it admiringly over an antique armchair.

Her white cotton night shirt fluttering about her shivering body, Beth continued her silent vigil as Cliff moved through the room. Her room. As he lifted, touched, rubbed her body. As he lifted, touched, rubbed himself.

"I like what you've done with this room, Beth. It's cozy. Warm. Inviting. I bet your clients like it, too."

Too terrified to move, to think, to respond, Beth stared silently at the monster who had so blatantly violated her home, her heart, and her life.

"So, that's the way it's going to be, huh? Silence. Well, that's okay. Actually, silence is good, very good. When the time comes, your silence will let me concentrate on me. And concentrating on me is always good. Speaking of good, I bet you're good Beth. Are you?"

Silence.

"I could ask your husband what he thinks, but then again, maybe he's never rocked your socks. Has he been? Has your big hulk of a husband ever rocked your socks?"

Silence.

Only inches away from Beth now, Cliff continued his taunting. His threatening. His planning.

"Don't worry, Beth. I'll rock your socks. And when I do, you will let me know, and then we will let the hulk know, okay? And how will we do that? Hmm, let's see. Oh, I know. Noise. We'll make some noise. Yes, you can let your hubby know how much fun you're having by making noise. Screams. Of course you'll scream. Won't you Beth? Your screams of delight will fill the night around us, Beth. Yes that's it. You'll scream. And I'll make sure of that."

That said, Cliff lunged at Beth. Grabbing at her breasts, Cliff managed to get a handful of her flimsy, cotton night shirt and with one good tug, he sent tiny pearl button, after tiny pearl button scattering across the whitewashed pine floor. Standing with the loose fabric still mercilessly draped over her shoulders, Beth dropped her head and looked at her body. A body she feared would never be the same after that night.

Really into it now, Cliff felt the welcome strain across his pants. He was hard, very hard, and very, very ready. He wanted her, and he would have her. But he wanted it to last. Forcing himself into neutral, Cliff stepped back and surveyed his beauty.

"You're shaking. Are you cold, Beth? Scared?"

Silence.

"Aw, come on Beth. You know what's gonna happen here. So, you might as well make the best of it."

"You're sick."

"Then 'shrink' me, doc. Make me better."

When Cliff's lunged for Beth this time, she managed to jump just beyond his reach.

Infuriated into a rage, Cliff spewed at his intended, "If you move away from me once more, I will stun you into submission. Got it?"

Nodding, Beth searched for the stun gun. Relief flooded through her when she found that it wasn't in his hand or in the waistband of his jeans.

Waistband! He had it in the waistband of his jeans. Maybe he put it in his jacket. Maybe, maybe...

"Hey, Beth, you looking for the stun gun? Don't worry I've still got it, right here in the back of my jeans. See?"

Beth's heart sank when her eyes found the stun gun nestled right next to a pistol, tucked tightly into the waistband of his jeans.

Lost in thought, Beth instinctively stepped back when Cliff made another move toward her.

"Tsk, tsk, Beth. You took a step without saying 'Mother may I'. Now you're gonna have to pay the piper."

~~ 59 ~~

As though playing a twisted game of mother may I, Cliff took one exaggerated step forward and pulled Beth close.

Pressed tightly against his body, there was no escaping Cliff's desire, his excitement. An excitement he ground into her flesh with every movement of his pelvis.

"Feel that, Beth. That's going to be yours, real soon."

A moan of fear escaped Beth's lips.

"That's right, Beth. You will moan. I'll make you moan, I'll make you cry, I'll make you scream with delight, too."

"Please, Mr. Jameson, don't."

"Mr. Jameson? I told you before, in my kitchen, remember. You can call me Cliff, Beth."

Silence.

Reaching behind her again, Cliff jerked her hair back until she looked into his eyes.

"I said call me Cliff."

"Cliff."

"That's right. Now let's move to the couch. It's time to play doctor."

"Noooo, please."
"You mean yes please, don't you?"

A cruel twist of fate allowed life to inch its way back into Philip's body, just as it seeped from his heart and soul.

Silently calling out to his wife, Philip willed her to live through her dance with evil. Willed her to return to him from the corners of hell.

Please Beth. Live. Please. And I'll live, too. We will be together, maybe start a family. Please Beth, live!

Beth's nightgown fell into a heap on the floor, as she fell into a heap beneath her attacker.

Hungrily, greedily, selfishly, Cliff covered her face with kisses. When he caught up with her mouth, he forced it open with his tongue. A tongue that slithered and slurped. A snake's tongue.

Beth! Disconnect! Focus on something outside of what's happening. Focus! Focus! Snake's tongue. Okay focus on that image.

Snakes.

I like snakes. Their movement, their independence.

Snakes. Yes snakes, and other reptiles, too. Think Beth! Think about anything, except what's going on right now. Think.

Frogs, swamps. Swamps, water, lush greens, thick with dew. Warm, moist, dew. Like in the rain forest.

Forest, animals. Lions, Tigers, and bears, oh my!

Just as Beth was about to spin off into Oz, she was brought back to reality by Cliff's sudden movement. Feeling his hand run along her breasts, and down toward her abdomen, Beth realized that her fate had been sealed. She was going to be raped. And Cliff Jamison was going to rape her. Just as soon as he freed himself from his jeans, he was going to rape her.

Struggling with his zipper, Cliff moved just far enough off Beth for her arms to loosen beneath him. Easing her right arm free, Beth dropped it toward the floor, left it there until Cliff moved his full weight back on top of her. As his hand searched for, and groped her panties away from her flesh, Beth made her move.

Hoping to distract her assailant, Beth let out a lusty moan. A moan that was answered by the pig on top of her. Forcing herself to move in unison with her rapist, Beth pressed her hips and thighs tight against him giving him very little wiggle room.

"Aw, good baby. I knew you'd like it."

Rock hard and ready, Cliff forced Beth's legs open and was just about to enter her, when Beth reached behind him, wrapped her hand around the handle of one of the guns tucked into the back of his jeans, aimed, and pulled the trigger.

As Beth pushed the lifeless form off her and on to the floor, her hysterical screams resonated throughout the tiny brick building.

"Philip! Philip! Help!"

"Beth, I'm cuffed, remember?"

"Cuffed? Yes."

Flying from the room, Beth threw herself onto her husband who welcomed her into his one free arm. Tenderly, gingerly touching his wife's naked body, Philip asked, "Beth. Jameson. What happened?"

"I used the stun gun on him."

"No, what happened?"

"Nothing"

"Something."

"No, Philip. I'm fine. Really."

"Okay. Look we don't have much time. We've got to get me out of these cuffs."

"Keys - we need the keys."

"Yes"

"Where are they?"

"I don't know. Probably in Jameson's pocket. You'll have to get them."

Without thinking, Beth ran back into the room. Cliff Jamison was right where she had left him. Flat on his back, unable to move, unable to speak, unable to cover his genitalia. His shriveled, pathetic genitalia.

Suddenly unsure of herself, Beth tentatively, cautiously moved toward the devil before her. Slight eyelid flutters let her know that he was alive, alive enough for another jolt. Beth picked up the stun gun, pulled the trigger, and sent another 50,000 volts of electricity through his body.

Her work with Cliff Jameson done, Beth hunted down the set of handcuff keys. She was thrilled when she found them in Jameson's jacket pocket. Was thrilled even more when they unlocked the cuffs binding the only man she had ever loved.

~~ 60 ~~

Wrapped tightly in Philip's plush terry robe, Beth followed her husband to the back room.

"What are we going to do?"

"First, we will cuff him."

"Then?"

"I don't know."

Statue-like, Beth watched Philip as he slapped the cuffs onto Cliff's wrists, as he zipped his jeans, as he took the pistol, as he lifted him onto the couch.

"Philip, we should call the police."

"I know."

"But, we're not going to?"

"Not yet."

From the expression on Philip's face, Beth could tell that he was struggling with his desire for revenge and his conscience. Allowing him time for his internal struggle Beth found herself with a little time to address feelings of her own.

Staring blankly at the man who had stripped her clothes from her, a man who planned to strip so much more from her, brought Beth to her knees. Trembling uncontrollably, Beth managed to push the loving intentions of her devoted husband away. Unfortunately, she was unable to push the perverted intentions of Denny's husband away. After a period of gut-wrenching pain, fear, and confusion filled the waning night around them, Beth turned pitiful eyes toward Philip.

"Beth, I don't know what to do. Tell me, please. What should I do?"

"Help me."

"How?"

"By loving me."

"I do."

"Still?"

"More than ever."

Kneeling beside his wife, Philip opened his arms and waited. He didn't have to wait long.

Several painfully quiet minutes past before Philip shared his plans with Beth. Plans, she soon learned, included two more rounds of electricity to immobilize Cliff Jamison. Plans that said loud and clear, that revenge proved victorious in Philip's internal battle against conscience.

Once pliable enough, Philip strung cord he had removed from Beth's blinds through Cliff's cuffs, led the cord underneath the length of the couch, then pulled it up around Cliff's ankles. After tying triple knots at both ends, Philip tried his creation by pulling on Cliff's feet.

Astonished, Beth watched as Cliff's hands and arms were pulled backward toward the floor with only the slightest pressure on Cliff's feet, just as his feet were pulled down and away when Philip tugged on his arms.

"Philip, you hog-tied him!"

"Sort of."

"Certainly seems appropriate."

"How so?"

"Hog-tying for the pig that he is."

Wincing from the pain of laughter, Philip allowed Beth to lead him back to the main house, and away from the man who had almost taken everything they had.

Each other.

Bolting upright in her bed, Denny pulled a series of short, choppy breaths into her lungs. Lungs that felt seared, scarred raw from the physical exertion of the past few hours as reality replace the lingering effects of the nightmare that had awakened her, Denny relaxed a bit in the stream of soft morning light filtering through antique lace curtains.

Beth's. I'm at Beth's house. Safe. Safe at Beth's.

"Beth!"

A deafening silence cut through the night around her.

"Beth!"

This time when silence greeted her, fear came along for the ride.

And almost uncontrollable sense of dread forced Denny from the safety of her bed, the safety of her room, and she went and search of

Beth and Philip. Weak like a kitten, and depending on corners of furniture for support, Denny slowly made her way to her bedroom door. Standing upright, Denny pulled the heavy door open, peaked into the still darkened hall and called for her friend once more.

"Beth!"

Countering her fear with the belief that all was well, Denny squared her shoulders and inched her way down the hall toward Beth's bedroom. Finding it empty, Denny's stepped into the tiny bathroom where Beth showered her, and peered out the daintily etched glass window at the circle driveway.

The 256indight blue Volvo and black BMW sitting quietly on the driveway announced that Beth and Philip hadn't abandoned her as she had feared. The presence of the vehicles, announced that all was well, because all seemed well. Turning from the breath-steamed window, Denny's eyes followed a steady stream of light pouring out from the small brick building in the back.

Beth? Philip? Are you guys out there? Alone?

Denny's unanswered questions, sent a ping of uncertainty and fear dancing along her insides.

Cliff, are you around here somewhere?

Her last question sent her in search of answers.

Waiting until she was a bit more steady on her feet, Denny devised a plan. A plan that had her venturing out to that small brick building, rather than waiting for Beth and Philip to come to her. Using the wall to help support her weight, she moved back into the hall and down the grand mahogany staircase. When she reached the final step, a paralyzing fear consumed her.

Security panel. The lights green. It's not on? They left me here in the house, alone, without the security system on? No. No. No. Something's wrong. Go back up. Go back up!

The opening of the back door, followed by a gust of air, sent Denny off the bottom step. Turning left into the far end of the kitchen, Denny ducked between Beth's antiques and waited.

"Beth, let's get cleaned up, then decide what we should do about Jameson."

"You're sure he can't get out of the ropes and handcuffs?"

"Yes."

"So, there's NO WAY he can get in here, right?"

"Not without help."

Wincing in pain with every upward step, Philip leaned tight against his pillar of strength.

"Beth."

"Yes?"

"I'm so glad you're alright."

"I know."

Crouched between an antique ladder-back chair and a turn-of-the-century baby stroller, Denny quickly grasped the situation.

Cliff's in the little brick building, roped and cuffed.

Perfect!

61

A gust of air let him know he was no longer alone.

"Help! I need help back here!"

Closing his eyes, Cliff quickly offered up a prayer that it would be anyone other than the hulk who came through the door. When he saw her standing in the doorway, he knew his prayers had been answered.

"Denny. Oh, thank God it's you. I was afraid it might be those two nuts who kidnapped you. Kidnapped you, and hog-tied me. Look, Denny. Look what they've done to me."

Slowly, very slowly, Denny's eyes took in the sights.

"See, Denny. I need help. Your help. Denny, look at me. Denny, my face, look at my face."

"Your face, yes, your face."

"That's right, Denny. Now move a little closer, okay?"

"Okay."

Inching her way toward her husband, Denny never once took her eyes from his. Never once broke his mesmerizing, hypnotizing stare.

"That's right, Denny. Help me. We've got to get out of here before they come back. When we get out of here, we'll go home, we'll start over. Things will be different Denny. I promise."

"Promise?"

"Yes."

"Yes, promise. That's good. Promise."

Leaning over Cliff, Denny struggled with the ropes that bound her husband's arms and hands. Struggled with the emotions that bound her to him, as well.

"That's right, Denny, the ropes. Loosen the ropes. If the ropes are off, I'll be able to get out. We can take care of the cuffs later."

"Right, ropes. Loosen the ropes."

"Yes, loosen the …"

Working the knot with her left hand, Denny tightened the fingers of her right hand around the stun gun she'd found on the bench in the mudroom. Then, with one fell swoop, Denny pushed Cliff's arms toward the floor, and pumped thousands of volts of electricity into her husband's neck. Stepping back to survey her work, Denny didn't find the sense of fulfillment she had hoped for. No, the effects of the stun gun proved only marginally satisfying.

More. I want more. I want …

Pushing her hands deep into Cliff's pant pockets, Denny rummaged around until she found what she wanted. What she needed.

Pills. Tiny, green pills.

Pulling a handful of green pills from the depths of his pockets, Denny quickly shoved them into Cliff's nearly paralyzed mouth. Pinching off his air-supply, Denny waited until gasps of air told her that the tiny, green pills had found their way down Cliff's throat.

Thrilled to the bone, Denny dropped to the floor, and sitting next to her husband, she waited. While she waited, she lovingly stroked her husband's cheek. His strong, determined, stunningly good-looking cheek. Just above a whisper, Denny talked tenderly to the man she had loved for so many years. The man she had willingly given herself to, the man with whom she bore children. The man she now wanted dead.

"Cliff, it didn't have to end like this, you know."

Finding Denny's room empty sent terrifying chills along their every nerve.

"Oh my God, Philip. Where is she?"

A frantic search of the upstairs didn't answer Beth's question conclusively, but it told them where Denny wasn't.

"Do you suppose she went downstairs?"

"She must have."

Grabbing hold of his wife's hand, Philip raced down the winding staircase toward the back door. Reaching for the gun he'd left on the mudroom bench, and finding the stun gun missing, Philip shot a knowing look at Beth when he realized where Denny had gone, and why she had gone there.

"Oh my God. Denny's out there. With him!"

Pulling his wife behind him, Philip bolted from the kitchen, across the driveway and into the brick building. Moaning in pain with every step, Philip pushed through, knowing they had to get to Denny quickly.

"Denny! Denny!"

Rewarded with a tiny, "Yes," Philip and Beth raced to the back room. An emotionally drained Denny sat curled up on the floor next to the couch that held her hog-tied husband. Her head supported by her bent knees, Denny casually waved Cliff's stun gun toward her visitors.

"Beth, I don't want you to come in."

"Why not?"

"Because we have things to do."

"We?"

"Cliff. Me."

"Denny, are you alright?"

"Yes."

"What are you doing?"

"Waiting."

"Waiting, for what?"

"For the pills to take effect."

"Pills, what pills?"

"The little green ones."

"Oh my God, Denny. You took pills? Please tell me you didn't."

"I didn't."

"Then, what do you mean?"

"Cliff."

"Cliff took pills?"

"Only when I made him."

62

Ignoring the stun gun and Denny's previous instructions, Beth rushed to Cliff's side. As she checked his vitals, she asked Denny a series of questions.

"Denny, how many pills?"

"I don't know."

"One? Two?"

"A handful."

"Oh Jesus! Philip, help me please."

"Help you what?"

"Loosen him."

"I will not! This man tried to kill all of us."

"Come on, Philip. We don't know what those pills are. They might kill him."

"And they might not have any affect on him at all. Until we're sure which it is, I'm not touching those ropes."

"Denny."

"Yes."

"What on earth did you think you'd accomplish by giving Cliff those pills? Were you trying to kill him?"

"Don't answer that, Denny."

"Oh for God's sake, Philip, stop playing defense lawyer, and help me out."

Crossing the room with two well-placed steps, Philip pulled his wife from Cliff's side, spun her toward him, then into the seat across from the couch.

"Beth, sit a minute. Think. Regroup."

Turning toward Denny, he continued, "Denny, tell me why you drugged Cliff."

"I want to ask him some questions. I figure the pills might make him answer honestly."

Turning an expectant, almost hopeful eye toward his wife, Philip asked, "Will they?"

"I don't know. Maybe. It's possible."

"Wow. Looks like we just found ourselves an ace in the hole."

Cliff stirred an hour or so later, and his captors were ready for him.

"Beth, turn on the recorder."

When the tiny wheels pumped life into the recorder, Philip identified the parties present and the purpose of the taping.

"This is Philip Malone. With me are Dr. Beth Malone, Denny Jameson, and her husband, Cliff Jameson. We are assembled in Dr. Malone's office so Mr. Jameson can come clean about recent events in his life. Is that an accurate statement, Mr. Jameson."

"Yes."

Tiny yelps of victory escaped Denny's mouth before Philip continued.

"Mr. Jameson, do you know where you are?"

"Yes."

"Can you tell me where you are?"

"Beth's office."

"Did you have an appointment with Dr. Malone?"

"No."

"So, you're an invited guest of Dr. Malone's?"

"No."

"Then how did you come to be at Dr. Malone's?"

"I broke in."

"Into her office?"

"No. Her house."

"Why did you break into her house, Mr. Jameson?"

"I wanted my wife back."

"Your wife?"

"Yes."

"Do you mean Denny?"

"Yes."

"Why did you want Denny back?"

"Because Dr. Malone kidnapped her and I wanted to get her back."

Realizing how incriminating that sounded, Philip quickly tried to establish the reason Beth took Denny.

"When you say kidnapped, do you mean she took Denny without your consent?"

"Yes."

"But she had your mother's consent and your wife's consent. Isn't that correct?"

"I don't know."

"Well that's the case, Mr. Jameson. Dr. Malone removed your wife from your home because your wife asked her to."

"If you say so."

"Mr. Jameson, do you know why Denny asked Dr. Malone to take her from your home?"

"No."

"Could you venture a guess as to why Denny asked Dr. Malone to take her from your home?"

"Yes."

"Why?"

"Because Denny figured out what I was doing."

"And, what did Denny figure out? What were you doing?"

"Drugging her."

"Why were you drugging her."

"Because I wanted her dead."

~~ 63 ~~

All eyes turned toward Denny. Her overwhelming need for answers however, seemed to deflect any pain Cliff's words should have caused her.

"Mr. Jameson, you wanted your wife, Denny, dead? Is that what you're saying?"

"Yes."

"Why?"

"So I could be with Sheila."

"Sheila? Who is Sheila?"

"My lover."

"You and Sheila were having an affair?"

"Yes."

"And, you wanted Denny out of the way?"

"Yes."

"Why not just get a divorce?"

"Because I wanted the kids, too. I knew I never would have gotten them unless I made Denny look like an unfit mother, or I killed her."

"That's why you began drugging her?"

"Yes."

"Tell me what happened when you drugged Denny."

"She started fucking up. Her behavior became erratic. Everyone noticed. The kids. My mother. The principal at the kid's school. They all thought she was nuts, or at least well on her way."

"So, your plan was to get her out of your life, not necessarily kill her?"

"No, eventually she'd end up dead."

"By your hand?"

"Maybe. But, I really think she would have offed herself when I got custody of the kids. So, either way, she'd be dead, and I would win."

Drawing Beth's attention from the monster before them, Philip whispered the words, "Watch Denny," before resuming his questioning. "So, if your plan had worked, you'd have taken the kids and started a new life with Sheila?"

"Yes."

"Did Sheila know about your plan when you began drugging Denny?"

"No."

"Does Sheila know about your plan now?"

Cliff laughed his response, "No."

"Why not? Why keep your plans to be with her a secret?"

"Sheila doesn't know anything anymore."

"What do you mean?"

"She doesn't know anything, because she's brain dead."

"What do you mean, brain dead?"

"You know; comatose."

"She's sick?"

"You could say that."

"She has an illness?"

Another laugh.

"Mr. Jameson, how did Sheila become 'brain dead' as you put it?"

"I shot her."

Those three little words hit Philip, Beth, and Denny with the blunt force of a bullet. Perhaps with as much force as the bullet Cliff sent into the head of his lover.

Congregating in Beth's outer office, they quickly assessed where they were, and where they were going.

"Philip, I'm not sure this matters, but Cliff came to me one night when he thought I was sleeping. He was upset — really upset. He was ranting and raving, said he'd done something that night that could jeopardize his entire future."

"You think that was the night he shot Sheila?"

"Yes."

"Beth, the shooting over at the high school. When was that?"

"I don't remember, but within the last few weeks."

"The victim's name, can you remember what it was?"

"Reddy, I think."

"Right! It was Sheila Reddy."

"Oh my God, Philip. He shot that poor woman?"

"Looks like it."

"That's it! We need to call the police, Philip. Now!"

"NO!"

"Denny, we have to."

"NO! Not until I have answers to MY QUESTIONS. Please Beth, Cliff's the only one who knows what happened, when it happened, and why it happened. If we call the cops now, they'll take him away and he'll never tell me. I'll spend the rest of my life searching for answers that I can get now. Please, let me try. Please, it's my only hope."

Against her better judgment, Beth followed her husband and her friend to the backroom. Committed to the philosophy of knowledge is power, Beth leaned against the wall, and silently waited for Denny to gain her knowledge.

In lawyer mode once again, Philip resumed his line of questioning about the school shooting.

"Mr. Jameson."

"Yes."

"I have a few more questions about Sheila."

"What?"

"You said you'd been having an affair with her."

"Yes."

"And you were going to take your children and live with her."

"Yes."

"So, what happened? Why did you decide to kill her?"

"I found someone new."

"Who?"

"Beth. Beth Malone."

Hearing her name coming from such a vile creature, Beth reacted as though she had been hit with 50,000 volts from his stun gun.

"That son-of-a-bitch!"

Blocked by Philip, Beth was forced to listen as Cliff recited his diabolical plan.

"And, in order to have Beth, you decided you first needed to get rid of Sheila. Is that right?"

"Yes."

"So, you shot her?"

"Yes."

"At the high school?"

"Yes."

"What did you do with the gun you shot her with?"

"Dumped it."

"Where?"

"Lake Chumgawanga."

Cliff's admission sent Philip, Beth and Denny scrambling to the front office once more.

"Okay, Philip. We have enough against him. We need to call the police."

Sensing Denny's mounting anxiety, Philip quickly devised a plan. A plan he hoped Denny would agree to.

"Denny, Beth's right. We have enough information now to go to the police and ensure a conviction."

"But ..."

"But you want your turn with Cliff?"

"Yes."

"Okay, how about this? What if we switch the tape in the recorder with a new one. We'll let you have a whack at getting answers from Cliff."

"I can ask him questions, and I can record him?"

"Yes."

"What about his taped confession?"

"I'll call the police department and ask to speak to the person in charge of the high school shooting investigation. I'll arrange to meet him, maybe play the tape for him. I'm sure he will want to talk with Cliff, but by that time, you should have what you want. Sound fair?"

"Yes."

"Okay, just let me make a quick call, then he's all yours."

While Philip placed his call, Beth and Denny waited in the outer sitting area. Denny's anxiety building with each passing moment.

"Beth."

"Yes?"

"I had a dream tonight. A nightmare, actually."

"Was it the same as the others?"

"No, the breakfast and forest scenes were missing from this dream."

"So, you stayed in your bedroom during the entire dream?"

"Yes."

"Was that significant?"

"Yes."

"Why?"

"Because the images of what happened in the bedroom that day were clearer."

"Really?"

"Yes."

"So, you know more about that last day?"

"Yes."

"Like what?"

"Remember when I told you I thought I called someone on the phone?"

"Yes."

"Well, I know now that I did call someone."

"Do you remember who you called?"

"No, but I'm hoping Cliff knows whether I called the school like I think I did. If he knows, and if he tells me, then at least I'll know I did everything I could to keep the kids at school and off the bus that day."

When Philip joined the women, he quickly updated them on his call and the message he left for the head of the investigation into Sheila Reddy's shooting.

"The desk sergeant said that Sgt. Carbone was handling the investigation. Today is his day off, but he said he would have him call me as soon as possible."

"Will he call today? Please Philip tell me he'll call today!"

"I can't imagine that he won't Beth. He wants to know who shot Principal Sheila Reddy, and I know who shot her. That was the message I left."

Looming over the foot of the couch, Philip hoped his presence would provide Denny a sense of security, in this less than secure world. Turning the tape recorder on, he motioned for Denny to begin.

"Cliff."

"What?"

"I want some answers."

"So."

"So, you'll give them to me."

"Fuck you, Denny!"

Concerned by the notable change in Cliff's tone and manner, Beth cautioned her friend, "Denny, the drugs may be wearing off. You'd better hurry."

"Oh, okay."

Deep in thought, Denny moved along Cliff's body, casually touching the man she'd once vowed to love forever. A heavy sigh seemed to punctuate the mood that enveloped her like an early spring fog. Tenderly caressing the face that had once held her dreams, Denny forced herself from the past and toward the future. A future that depended on her finding out the truth.

*Truth — I **need** the truth. I **deserve** the truth.*

To ensure her quest, Denny slipped her hand into her bathrobe pocket and pulled the last of the tiny green pills forth. Lunging onto her husband's body, she quickly popped them into his mouth and pinched his nostrils closed once again.

"Denny! Don't!"

Before Beth or Philip could pull Denny from Cliff's body, some of the pills made their way down his throat.

~~ 65 ~~

There were no words spoken, no apologies made during Cliff's tumble down his drug-induced road to hell. As Denny waited for Cliff to bottom out, she mindlessly paced Beth's cozy little haven. Her pacing led her to Beth's discarded nightgown.

"Beth, your nightgown. It's ripped."

"Yes."

"How did it get ripped? Beth, how did it get ripped?"

Answering her own question with a menacing glare toward Cliff, "He did this to you, didn't he?"

"Yes."

"Did he …"

"No."

"But he tried, didn't he?"

"Yes."

"God, Beth he tried to rape you, almost killed Philip and me, and you're upset with me because I gave him a little taste of his own medicine?"

"Not upset, Denny. Concerned, that's all. God Denny, don't you think I'd like to pump him full of drugs, or bullets?"

"You would?"

"Of course. I'm not a saint, you know."

"Maybe not a saint — but a savior."

Cliff's moan made Denny's skin crawl and her heart plummet. Knowing what she knew about her husband, Denny silently wished that he would die at her hand.

"Cliff."

"What?"

"I want to talk to you."

"About what?"

"About the pills."

A short laugh escaped Cliff, a laugh that told Denny she was in for quite a ride.

"Cliff!"

"What?"

"When did you start drugging me?"

"When the kids went back to school from summer vacation."

Quietly thinking back, Denny concluded the timing was right.

"Last September? You began drugging me last September?"

"Yes."

"When did you give me the drugs?"

"In the mornings."

"How?"

"In your coffee."

"What did you give me?"

"Whatever shit I got on drug busts."

"You don't even know what you gave me?"

"Don't know and I don't care. What's the difference?"

"Cliff, the kids. I drove the kids back and forth to school, for God's sake."

"I know."

"You put the kids in danger every time you gave me a pill."

"Fuck you, Denny. I never drugged you until after you dropped the kids, and even then, I only gave you what I thought was enough to incapacitate you."

"Oh well then, I guess there's no problem."

"Sure there is."

"What?"

"You're still alive."

"Right, but Page and Preston aren't, are they, Cliff? They're dead, Cliff. And, I'm still alive. Alive! But your kids are dead. Page and Pres are D-E-A-D!"

The moan Denny had heard countless times come from the darkness inside her, suddenly came from her husband. Still Denny continued her torment.

"Cliff. Hey Cliff!"

"What?"

"Remember when you told me all those times that it was my fault the kids died in that accident?"

"Yeah."

"Well, it wasn't my fault, was it?"

"Yes."

"Really, Cliff? How's it my fault that the kids are dead?"

"You didn't pick the kids up from school."

"Because I couldn't. You made sure I couldn't. Remember!"

"Shut up, Denny."

"No! It's your fault the kids are dead, Cliff."

"Shut the fuck up, Denny!"

"Your fault — and **only your fault**!"

"No Denny, it's your fault, because if you'd died like you were supposed to, the kids would still be here. So you see Denny, it's your fault. All of it. Page, Pres, Shelia, they all paid a price. **Because you just wouldn't die!**"

~~ 66 ~~

"You're right, Cliff, I didn't die. But you're going to!"

Pulling the stun gun from under the couch, Denny threw herself onto Cliff before Philip or Beth could do anything to stop her.

When Philip grabbed the stun gun from Denny, he was happy to note its battery was so low that it didn't deliver much of a shock to Cliff. He felt the combination of the drugs and what shock he just received was enough. It was time to dial things back a bit.

Agitated to the point of hysteria, Beth addressed Denny, "Jesus, Denny! Why did you do that?"

"Because he lied."

"What? When?"

"When he said it was my fault the kids died."

"We know, Denny. It wasn't your fault, it was a tragic accident."

"My kids didn't have to be in that accident!"

"You mean if you'd picked them up. But you know it wasn't your fault you couldn't get to the school."

"No! I mean if Cliff had picked them up!"

"What, Denny? I don't understand."

"Remember when I told you my dream became clearer last night?"

"Yes."

"And that I wasn't sure who I called."

"Yes."

"Well, I wasn't completely honest with you."

"Does that mean you remember who you called?"

"Yes."

"But you didn't want to tell me? Why wouldn't you tell me?"

"Because I wanted to see if Cliff would confess."

"Confess what?"

"That I called him. That I told him **I couldn't** get the kids. That I asked him to go pick them up."

"What?"

"That's right, the phone call I made? Well, it was to Cliff."

"Denny, oh my God, are you certain?"

"Absolutely positive."

"Cliff didn't go get Page and Pres? Why?"

"Does it matter? He didn't get them, and they were killed by a train. It doesn't matter to me why he didn't get them. Nothing about him matters to me anymore. What does matter — and this matters a lot — **it's not my fault that Page and Pres were on the bus that day!**"

After making Denny and Beth promise not to uncuff Cliff under any circumstances, Philip left for his meeting with Sgt. Carbone.

Hoping that the amiable-looking man pacing the lobby of the police station was the man he planned to meet, Philip forced himself to swallow his fear. Cops could sense fear, and he knew he couldn't accomplish what he needed to accomplish if Carbone smelled fear.

"Sgt. Carbone?"

"Mr. Malone, what can I do for you?"

"Nothing, but I can do quite a lot for you."

"Really? And, what exactly can you do for me?"

"I can tell you who shot Principal Sheila Reddy."

"So your message said. Malone, why don't we go into my office and talk about what you know."

"I'd rather talk outside. In my car."

Sticking the tips of his fingers into the pockets of his jeans, Sgt. Carbone moved his jacket just enough so Philip could see the service revolver strapped to his shoulder.

"Carbone, I'm not carrying. I don't have any concealed weapons in my car."

"Good."

"But I do have what you need."

"Yeah, and what's that?"

"A confession. A taped confession."

Philip had expected a reaction from Carbone in the lobby of the station when he said he knew the identity of the high school shooter, but he got none. Sure he would receive one when Carbone heard Cliff Jamison identified as the person who was about to come clean, Philip watched intently for a reaction. When he received nothing from Carbone, Philip angrily flicked off the tape recorder.

"You're not surprised about Jameson?"

"Nope."

"Are you telling me he's a suspect?"

"I'm not telling you anything, Mr. Malone."

"Right."

"But you do know Jameson's a cop, right?"

"Yeah, I know. Not exactly one of your department's finest, I must say!"

"Just checking."

Desperate to hide the nervous energy searing through him, Philip pushed fast forward, moving the tape past anything that identified Cliff's current whereabouts. Then he pushed play once again, letting Cliff's voice take over inside the BMW.

~~ 67 ~~

As though in a vacuum, Philip and Sgt. Carbone listened as the devil incarnate threw himself into the fires of hell with his drug induced confession.

"Mr. Jameson, do you know why Denny asked Dr. Malone to take her from your home?"

"No."

"Could you venture a guess as to why Denny asked Dr. Malone to take her from your home?"

"Yes."

"Why?"

"Because Denny figured out what I was doing."

"And, what did Denny figure out? What were you doing?"

"Drugging her."

"Why were you drugging her."

"Because I wanted her dead."

"Mr. Jameson, you wanted your wife, Denny, dead? Is that what you're saying?"

"Yes."

"Why?"

"So I could be with Sheila."

"Sheila? Who is Sheila?"

"My lover."

It wasn't until Cliff identified Sheila Reddy as his lover that Sgt. Carbone showed any emotion, and even then, it was just a flicker. Paying attention, once again, to the words spilling forth from the tape, Philip knew it was only a matter of time before Carbone's flicker of recognition became a burning inferno.

"You and Sheila were having an affair?"

"Yes."

"And, you wanted Denny out of the way?"

"Yes."

"Why not just get a divorce?"

"Because I wanted the kids, too. I knew I never would have gotten them unless I made Denny look like an unfit mother, or I killed her."

"That's why you began drugging her?"

"Yes."

"Tell me what happened when you drugged Denny."

"She started fucking up. Her behavior became erratic. Everyone noticed. The kids. My mother. The principal at the kid's school. They all thought she was nuts, or at least well on her way."

"So, your plan was to get her out of your life, not necessarily kill her?"

"No, eventually she'd end up dead."

"By your hand?"

"Maybe. But, I really think she would have offed herself when I got custody of the kids. So, either way, she'd be dead, and I would win."

Raising his hand, Carbone signaled for Philip to stop the tape before speaking. "Look, Malone, I'm not sure what you've got going here, but I have to tell you, you're getting in pretty deep."

"I know."

"But, you're gonna go forward?"

"Yes."

"Okay, let's see what you've got."

Unable to heed the screams of caution bouncing through his head Philip pressed play. Somehow the word 'play' had lost all of its implied fun and games.

"So if your plan had worked, you'd have taken the kids and started a new life with Sheila?"

"Yes."

"Did Sheila know about your plan when you began drugging Denny?"

"No."

"Does Sheila know about your plan now?"

Cliff laughed his answer, "No."

"Why not?"

Philip's eyes never left Carbone's face. Stone cold and difficult to read, Philip was still able to register the slightest awareness in the seasoned professional. He knew what was coming, still Philip knew the officer would be shocked by Jameson's cold, harsh words.

"Sheila doesn't know anything anymore."

"What do you mean?"

"She doesn't know anything, because she's brain dead."

"What do you mean, brain dead?"

"You know; comatose."

"She's sick?"

"You could say that."

"She has an illness?"

Another laugh.

Cliff's laugh sucker-punched Carbone, his next words finished him off.

"Mr. Jameson, how did Sheila become 'brain dead' as you put it?"

"I shot her."

This time, it was Sgt. Carbone who turned the tape off. His hard as stone eyes slowly scanned the parking lot while his options tore through his mind.

With little to no options, Philip waited for Carbone's decision. It wasn't until Carbone spoke that Philip knew he'd probably be alright.

"Malone. As in Philip Malone? The defense attorney?"

"Yes."

"Okay Mr. Defense Attorney, is Jameson a client of yours?"

"Absolutely not."

"Will he be?"

"Good God, no!"

"Why not?"

"Because Cliff Jameson hurt someone I love. After you've heard the tape — the entire tape — you'll understand why I'd never defend a piece of shit like Jameson."

~~ 68 ~~

Philip patiently waited for Carbone to process what he'd heard. Waited for him to process his options. The wait was long, and it was necessary.

"Malone."

"Yeah?"

"Where's Jameson?"

"I can't tell you. At least not yet."

"Listen, I can get out of this car right now and I'll find Jameson. You obviously know exactly where he is, and you know I have a pretty good idea. So, what's the hold up? Why are you jerking me along?"

"I need something."

"What?" Carbone acted like that simple question caused him physical pain.

"Protection."

"Protection from whom?"

"Not who, more what?"

"Okay, from what?"

"Prosecution."

With that one little word, Philip opened himself, Beth, and Denny up to the scrutiny of Sgt. Carbone.

"You know I can't make any deals, Attorney Malone, but let's say I could, what would you say?"

"I'd say that things got a little out of control in my pursuit of justice."

"Your banged-up face already said that."

"My banged-up face happened immediately after Jameson broke into my house and forced me at gunpoint to my wife's office and then proceeded to use his stun gun on me several times."

"So tell me, Malone, how's Jameson look right about now?"

"Not too good, I'm afraid."

"Okay, so you two got into a little tussle, so what?"

"Well, the tussle's just the beginning."

"Okay, Malone, spill it."

"After Jameson rendered me unconscious, he went after my wife. He attempted to rape her. However, she is a tough one and managed to get his stun gun and incapacitate him, and uncuff me.

"Then we cuffed him and tied him up and went to clean ourselves up. While we were in the house, we discovered Denny Jameson was missing. We found her with him. She found him tied up and she drugged him with some of the same pills he had used on her. She got them from his own pocket.

"In a nut shell, the three of us are guilty of holding someone against their will, assault with a slightly less than deadly weapon, and drugging. Those are just the biggies. Add to that the fact that these offenses were committed against an officer of the law and I'm sure you'll reach the same conclusion I have. We are in some serious hot water."

Carbone sat quietly for a moment and then said, "Hot water? Nah, boiling, maybe!"

"Look Carbone, there are plenty of reasons why we did what we did. So, I'm hoping you're more interested in solving the homicide than you are in what we did to help you solve it."

"I hate to tell you Malone, but what I've heard so far won't help me solve shit. In fact, just knowing that Jameson was drugged when he made his confession makes me question whether anything on that tape's worth a shit."

"It is."

"Yeah? Well then dazzle me Mr. Malone, because so far you haven't!"

"Would knowing the location of the gun Jameson used on Principal Reddy dazzle you?"

"Razzle and dazzle me."

"Good. Then we've got a deal?"

"Yeah, deal. So, Mr. Lawyer, how's the deal gonna work?"

"Three people are going to give you statements about what happened."

"And."

"And, when they do, they will do so without having had their Miranda rights read to them."

"So those statements are inadmissible in court."

"Right."

"And, the gun? When will I get the gun?"

"Whenever you want it."

When Sgt. Carbone saw what had happened to Cliff Jamison at the hands of people who had been pushed beyond their limits, he had a momentary doubt about the deal he had made.

"God damn, Malone. He's practically dead." Philip thought momentarily about offering an explanation, but he soon realized that no words could ever adequately explain their dance with evil. So, he offered nothing. Least of all, an apology.

~~ 69 ~~

A few well-placed calls by Philip to friends throughout the legal community, left Cliff Jameson's defense up to a public defender. A public defender who had no doubt heard Cliff's opinion that all defense attorneys were scum.

Denny was sitting in the front row between her new best friends, Philip and Beth, and with her mother-in-law, Susan. They all looked on as the charges were read against her husband. While she knew Cliff could never be charged with the deaths of her children, just hearing the words, *knowingly drugged his wife into a crippling state, a state that prohibited her from retrieving her children from school that day — the same day Preston James and Page Susan Jameson lost their lives,* gave Denny a euphoric sense of victory. Almost as euphoric feeling as when Cliff pleaded Not Guilty by reason of insanity.

In stark contrast to the wants and wishes of victims' families across this country, Denny, Beth, and Philip were thrilled to the core by Cliff's insanity plea.

Sitting in the crowded courtroom that summer day, they silently but collectively prayed that the justice system would prevail. They all prayed the justice system would sentence Cliff to unlimited years of psychiatric evaluations, and court-appointed therapy, administered from within the walls of a maximum security mental institution.

And if Denny was granted her ultimate wish, the court-appointed therapy would include years of drug and electric shock therapy, too.

At the end of the day Denny said goodbye to Beth and Philip and took Susan home. While Denny viewed Cliff as nothing but a monster, he was still Susan's son. Denny knew her mother-in-law loved her, but she also knew Susan needed time to heal. And for the first time in months, Denny wanted to help Susan do just that.

About the Author

Sheryll O'Brien considered herself a storyteller, never a writer. However, she surprised her vast audience with the skill with which she crafted her stories. In the last three years of her life, she had over 30 books published, and became a multi-award-winning author.

Her first love was her family; her husband, their two daughters, her granddaughter, her mother, sister, and brother, in-laws and many, many friends. Her love of family was evident in the stories she told so well.

In 2022, Sheryll lost her battle with cancer, and the world lost a true talent. Several of her early works, including this one, were published posthumously.

If you have enjoyed Dancing with Evil, please consider posting a review on amazon.com and goodreads.com. Reviews help other readers make their choice on what to read next.

For more information on Sheryll O'Brien's works please visit her website -

pullingthreadsnovella.com

www.ingramcontent.com/pod-product-compliance
Lightning Source LLC
Chambersburg PA
CBHW071111250626
47159CB00002B/699